GIVE ME BACK MY BODY!

My legs straightened. I stood up. I turned away from the table. My legs carried me out of the cafeteria.

I wasn't controlling my body at all. Pete was.

No! I protested. *I won't go! You can't make me!*

I tried to stop walking. To plant my feet on the floor. But my feet wouldn't do what I told them to do. They kept going.

Stop! I shouted to myself.

I grabbed the door of the cafeteria. My legs kept walking, pulling me out. I clung to the door frame.

What do you want, Pete? I demanded silently.

What are you going to make me do?

R.L. Stine's
Ghosts of Fear Street® #28

HIDE
AND
SHRIEK
II

A Parachute Press Book

A GOLD KEY PAPERBACK
Golden Books Publishing Company, Inc.
New York

A GOLD KEY Paperback Original
Golden Books
888 Seventh Avenue
New York, NY 10106

Copyright © 1998 by Parachute Press, Inc.

Hide And Shriek II written by Emily James

ISBN: 0-307-24900-X

First Gold Key paperback printing March 1998

10   9   8   7   6   5   4   3   2   1

Cover art by Jim Ludtke

Printed in the U.S.A.

Chapter ONE

Happy birthday to me,
   Happy birthday to me . . .
   My birthday is coming. It's only two weeks away.
   I love my birthday. Every year I play hide-and-seek
with all my friends. And the best part is—I always
win.
   Well—almost always.
   The kids think they're safe this year. They
think they got rid of me.
   But it's not that easy to get rid of Pete.
   I'm trapped in this graveyard—for now. But I'll find
a way out.
   And when I do . . .
   Ready or not. Here I come.

"Ready for lunch, Becky?" Darcy Noonan asked me. She gathered her books from the top of her desk.

I checked my schedule. Yep. Time for lunch.

"Come on," Darcy said, standing. "I'll show you where the cafeteria is."

As we left the classroom, I stopped her. Kids streamed around us through the hallway of Shadyside Middle School. "Wait—I'll bet I can find the cafeteria myself," I declared. I lifted my nose in the air and sniffed. "Peas and carrots—succotash," I announced. "I can find the cafeteria just by the smell."

Darcy laughed. "Don't get thrown off the trail by Brian," she warned, pointing at a greasy-looking kid down the hall. "He wears *eau de succotash* cologne."

I smiled, even though I thought her comment was a little mean. I liked Darcy. We met in class at the beginning of the day. Darcy sits in the seat next to mine.

It was my first day at Shadyside Middle School. My family had just moved to town.

Lots of kids said hi to Darcy as we headed for the cafeteria. She seemed to know everybody. She's pretty—tall and athletic, with long, shiny brown hair.

"Isn't it hard starting a new school at the end of May?" she asked me. "I mean, everybody already knows each other. And you have to take tests on stuff you never even learned."

I shrugged. "It's no big deal."

Actually, it wasn't any big deal. My dad's a scientist. He moves around a lot for his work, and my family moves with him. So I'm used to making new friends. I try to be nice to everyone—and they're usually nice back.

The cafeteria was huge and crowded. Kids scrambled for places to sit. I spotted Max Fisher, who lives next door to me. He was sitting with a girl I didn't know.

"There's a seat over there." I pointed out Max's table to Darcy.

She shrugged and said, "Whatever."

Max grinned when he saw us coming. He's tall and skinny, with frizzy brown hair that falls in his eyes. The day we moved into our new house, Max came over to say hi. "I'm so glad you moved in," he told me. "This weird old lady lived here before you. She used to throw spitballs at me every time I walked by."

"Wow," I said. "What happened to her?"

"She died," he said, as if it were no big deal.

Now I pulled my brown lunch bag out of my backpack and sat beside Max.

"Hi, Becky. Hi, Darcy," he greeted us.

"Hi," the girl across from him mumbled. She was very pale and thin, with straight black hair that hid her face like a veil.

3

"This is Mina Baird," Darcy told me. She rolled her eyes. I figured Darcy thought Mina was kind of strange. And I have to say, with all that hair in front of her face, Mina looked pretty freaky. But since it was my first day, I decided to keep an open mind about her.

"Hi, Mina." I smiled. "I'm Becky Tabor."

Mina nodded.

I opened my lunch bag and started eating. I packed my own lunch—chicken salad on whole wheat and an orange. I've been packing my own lunch since I was six. My mom makes the worst lunches—baloney and ketchup sandwiches are her specialty. Yuck!

I bit into my sandwich and stared at a huge calendar on the cafeteria wall. It showed the months of May and June. One date—June tenth—was circled in red.

"June tenth," I wondered out loud. "Is that the last day of school?"

"I wish," Darcy grumbled. "School doesn't end for another month."

"The last day is the twenty-sixth," Max added.

"So what's June tenth?" I asked.

Darcy pointed beneath the calendar. "See what that says?"

At the bottom of the calendar someone had printed 14 MORE DAYS UNTIL PETE'S BIRTHDAY.

The number could be changed as the days passed. Someone had scribbled graffiti around the sign. YEAH—IF HE SHOWS UP. Someone else had written WHAT A JOKE, and OOOO—I'M SCARED.

"Who's Pete?" I asked.

"Nobody," Mina replied quietly.

Nobody? He sure didn't seem like nobody. "Well, what's all this stuff about his birthday?" I went on. "Is it some kind of big party or something?"

Darcy flicked my question away. "It's nothing," she insisted. "It's just a dumb game. I'm too old for that silly stuff."

"You're twelve," Mina said. "Just like the rest of us."

Darcy stared at her for a second. "I *know* that, Mina," she said. "But I still say it's stupid."

I bit into an orange slice and stared at the calendar. It takes a while to get used to a new school, I told myself. It'll all make sense to me soon, I guess.

I rode my bike home from school that afternoon. I pedaled slowly so I could glance around me. I'd lived in Shadyside for only three days, so I wanted to check out the town.

The sun warmed my back as I rode. Not a bad place, I thought.

Then I turned onto my new street, Fear Street. Suddenly, the sun seemed to disappear. I felt chilly.

Fear Street was lined with tall, old trees that blocked the sun.

I passed a beautiful mansion towering beyond locked gates. A few yards past the mansion stood a huge Victorian house. It was painted about ten different colors and was missing a few shingles. Farther down the road I saw a square brick house with no windows.

There sure are some strange houses on this street, I thought. Who lives in these places anyway?

I moved closer to my house. On my right I saw a fancy iron fence. Beyond the fence—the Fear Street Cemetery.

I shivered. I'm normally pretty logical—like my dad. I know there's nothing to really be afraid of in a cemetery. But still, for some weird reason, cemeteries give me the creeps.

I started pedaling faster. I pulled close to a bunch of bushes inside the cemetery gate.

Suddenly, the bushes moved.

There was no wind that day. Not one breeze. Fear Street was completely still and quiet.

And still, with no breeze, the bushes shook harder. Something was in there—hiding!

From inside the shrubbery, a horrible sound ripped through the air—a terrible, chilling howl!

shuddered. I wanted to ride away as fast as I could—but I froze.

Aaaaooooohhh!

That piercing howl again!

The bushes shook even harder. I've got to get out of here! I thought. I started to pedal away.

Then a lump caught in my throat.

Something leapt out of the bushes!

It was a dog. I sighed with relief.

Aaaaooooooh! the mutt wailed. I stopped and shook my head. "How dumb can you get?" I scolded myself. "It's only a dog!"

The dog slipped between the iron bars of the gate. It ran up to me and sniffed my hand. It was a short, patchy brown-and-white dog with stubby legs.

"What's the matter with you?" I asked it. "What's making you howl like that?"

The dog licked my fingers. I petted it. It didn't seem hurt or anything.

"You sure you're all right?" I said.

The dog wagged its thumb-sized tail.

Whew. I patted my chest to make my heart stop pounding. All that nervousness for nothing!

"Well, nice meeting you. Take care, dog," I called. I rode away, glancing at the sky. I'd better hurry home, I thought. Through the trees I could see storm clouds gathering.

Thunder rumbled in the distance as I pulled into my driveway. For a Fear Street house, ours was pretty normal. It was made of brown shingles, two stories high. The paint was chipped in places, but my parents were planning to fix it up.

I parked my bike in the garage and went inside. My little sister, Martha, sat at the kitchen table. A big red kite lay on the floor. Martha was tying a key to the kite string.

"Where's Mom?" I asked.

"She went to the store," Martha replied.

"What are you doing?"

"I'm going to discover electricity," she told me.

I reached for the light switch and flicked several times. "I hate to break it to you, Martha, but look!"

8

The kitchen light blinked on and off. "Electricity has already been discovered."

"Well, then, I'm going to *re*discover it," she sniffed.

Martha's nine. She thinks she's the reincarnation of Benjamin Franklin. Really.

She looks kind of like him, I guess. She's a little chubby, with straight brown hair that she always ties back in a ponytail. She even wears little silver-framed glasses.

I'm taller and skinnier, and I keep my hair short. But otherwise I look like Martha, I guess. My mom says we both have Dad's round, honest brown eyes.

Another rumble of thunder, louder than the last one.

"Storm's a-comin'," Martha said in her dopey Ben Franklin talk. "Tonight's the night. I've got to get ready. This discovery will change the world!"

"Oh, brother," I sighed.

I heard Mom's car pull into the driveway. "Mom's home," Martha announced, as if I didn't know. "By the way, 'Nothing can be said to be certain except death and taxes.'"

"What?"

She glared at me impatiently. "Don't you remember the code?"

"Oh, yeah." When we were younger, Martha and I made up a code. She knows a lot of Ben Franklintype sayings by heart, so we used them for a secret code. "A penny saved is a penny earned" meant "I just sneaked a cookie from the kitchen." "Well done is better than well said" meant "If you tell on me, I'll kill you."

"What does 'death and taxes' mean again?" I asked.

"It means Mom's in a bad mood," she whispered just before Mom came through the door.

"Hi, girls," Mom chirped. She put a bag of groceries on the counter. Then she gave me a kiss hello. "How did school go today?"

She didn't seem to be in a bad mood at all. "Death and taxes don't seem very certain to me, Martha," I commented.

"Well, they *were* when she left," Martha snapped.

"What are you two talking about?" Mom asked. "Is this that code again?"

Martha tried to act innocent. "Huh? What code?"

Mom gave a little smirk and shrugged. "Never mind. Becky, would you mind putting the groceries away for me? I'm going upstairs for a minute. Then I want to hear all about your first day at school."

"Okay, Mom," I agreed. I reached into the grocery bag and pulled out a box of cereal. Then I stopped for a minute, uncertain. "Which cabinet does the cereal go in?" I asked her.

"Put it anywhere you like. We're starting from scratch!" Mom smiled and left the kitchen.

"Did you make any new friends today?" I asked Martha.

"Yeah. I met this girl, Beth. She's pretty nice."

"That's good." I watched Martha struggle with her knots on the string for a second. Then I opened an empty cabinet and started filling it with cereal boxes.

"Are you playing in that game, Becky?" Martha asked.

"What game?"

"That special game they have here. Everybody who's twelve has to play," Martha explained. "Beth told me about it. Her big sister played last year."

"I don't know what you're talking about," I said. But something did ring a bell. I remembered the calendar in the cafeteria—and Mina telling Darcy, "You're twelve, just like the rest of us."

"What else did Beth say?" I asked. "Did she mention anybody named Pete?"

Martha shook her head. "Nope. That's all I know." She picked up her kite and headed for the back door. "I'm going outside to get my experiment ready. 'Time is money,' you know."

"Mom, when can we have roast goose for dinner?" Martha whined. "I'm really hungry for roast goose."

Mom forked some salad onto Martha's plate. "How can you be hungry for roast goose?" she asked. "You've never tasted it."

"Yes, I have," Martha insisted. "In my past life."

Mom, Dad, and I all groaned at once. Martha really took this Ben Franklin stuff too seriously.

Dad snapped open the newspaper. "Why don't you think about your future for a change, Martha? Let's see: 'Aries—New friends bring fun into your life. But don't let your work slide, or you'll find yourself in trouble.' Sounds to me like you better hit the books, young lady."

Dad reads our horoscopes to us every night at dinner. Which really annoys me, because my dad's usually so logical. And horoscopes are so silly. He's a scientist. You'd think he'd be too sensible to believe in astrology. But no.

"Want to hear yours, Capricorn?" he asked me.

"Don't bother. Just pass the spaghetti, please."

Every night I tell Dad I didn't want to hear my horoscope. And every night he reads it to me anyway.

"'A period of transition, Capricorn. You won't be feeling quite yourself these days. Don't let outside forces overwhelm you. All eyes are on you now.' Hmm. That's interesting—especially since you're starting a new school."

"Come on, Dad," I protested. "That horoscope could work just as well for Martha, or you or Mom. It doesn't mean anything."

"I disagree," Dad said. "We're part of the universe,

and the universe is part of us. Why shouldn't the stars affect us as much as the weather?"

Just then thunder rumbled outside. Martha perked up.

"Eat your spaghetti, Martha," Mom chided. "I'm sure Ben Franklin liked spaghetti just as much as roast goose."

"No, he did not," Martha countered. "I don't want to eat too much tonight anyway. A full belly makes a dull brain."

"Martha," Dad said wearily. "Just eat."

After dinner I finished my homework and went downstairs to watch TV. I stopped in the kitchen for a glass of juice. Thunder rolled and boomed outside. The storm was getting close.

I glanced out the kitchen window. There was Martha with her kite. She was tossing it into the wind, trying to get it to fly.

I shook my head. What a nut. How could a sensible kid like me have such a weirdo for a sister?

Oh, well. The rain would start pouring down soon. That would send her inside.

I took my juice into the living room. Mom and Dad sat on the couch, watching some boring news show.

The lights and the TV flickered off. A huge bolt of lightning cracked through the sky. Thunder came crashing after it.

The hair on the back of my neck prickled.

Then an ear-splitting scream ripped through the darkness!

"That came from the backyard!" Mom cried.

I ran to the kitchen and threw the back door open. Outside, a figure was crumpled on the ground, clutching a kite.

I gasped.

"Oh, no! Martha!"

Chapter THREE

Martha and her stupid experiment! I thought in a panic. She must have electrocuted herself!

Mom and Dad followed me out to the backyard. "Martha!" I shouted. "Are you all right?"

I ran to her, grabbed her by the shoulders, and shook her. "Did you hurt yourself?"

The rain poured down on us. Martha's eyes fixed on the trees that bordered the yard. "I saw some-one!" she cried. "Out there! Someone's watching me!"

"What?" I stared through the darkness. The trees rustled. Was it the wind? Or was someone moving out there?

"I'm sure it's just a shadow," Mom said. "Calm down, Martha."

Dad helped Martha to her feet. "What were you doing on the ground?" he demanded. "Much less out in the storm!"

"I slipped in the mud," she explained. "I—"

The trees rustled again. We all stopped to listen.

I didn't think it was a shadow. I splashed through the wet grass to get a better look.

The trees moved again. I heard footsteps!

"Someone *is* there!" I shouted. I chased after the person. The spy crashed through a row of bushes.

"Hey! You!" I shouted.

But the spy disappeared in the shadows.

"Becky, get back here!" Dad called.

We all ran inside to get out of the rain. The lights flickered back on.

"Martha, what were you doing out there?" Dad demanded. "You could've been hurt!"

"I was discovering electricity, Dad," Martha explained. "It's very important."

"I saw someone!" I insisted. "Someone *was* spying on Martha."

"It couldn't be," Mom said. "Who would do such a thing?"

"Maybe it was a British spy, trying to steal my scientific secrets!" Martha cried.

"It could've been an animal or something," Mom suggested. "Girls, go dry yourselves off. There are clean towels in the closet."

"Mom! What about the spy!" Martha said.

Cupping his hand around his eyes, Dad peered out the window. Another crack of lightning lit up the yard.

"Whoever—or whatever—was out there is gone now," he said. "I'm sure it was nothing. Besides, why would anybody have any reason to spy on us?"

That was a logical question to ask. And Mom was right. No one had any reason to spy on us. But, still, I had a funny feeling. I was sure I saw somebody—and whoever it was, they didn't want to be caught.

"And you really think someone was spying on you?" Darcy asked. She folded her lunch bag into a neat square. We were sitting together in the cafeteria. I was telling her about what had happened the night before.

I shrugged. "I don't know what to think. All I know is, someone was out there."

"You should be careful," Darcy warned. "You live on Fear Street, right?"

I nodded.

"Well, I don't really *believe* in this stuff or anything—" Darcy shifted in her seat. "But—you know—it's a weird part of town. I'd never let *my* parents move there."

"What's weird about it?" I asked.

"I've heard stories—they're probably not true or

anything—but—you know, they're about ghosts and stuff."

"I don't believe in ghosts," I explained. "My sister does, but I don't."

"And there's Pete," Darcy went on. "He lived on Fear Street."

"Pete?" I echoed. My ears pricked up at the sound of the familiar name. "Where does he live now?"

Darcy gave me a funny look. "He's—um—he's not around anymore."

I found myself staring at the calendar as I finished my lunch. June tenth. Pete's birthday. Who was this Pete guy anyway? Did that have anything to do with the game Martha was talking about?

Darcy left to do some homework in the library. I wandered outside. It was another warm, sunny May day—one of those days that feels as if nothing bad could ever happen.

Max was sitting on a bench near the water fountain. I sat down beside him.

"Hi, Max," I said. Then I got right down to business. "What's that calendar in the cafeteria for? What's going to happen on June tenth?"

"June tenth is Pete's birthday," Max replied.

"I know, but who's Pete? Does he go to school here? And what's going to happen on his birthday?" I demanded. Why wouldn't anyone give me a straight answer about this?

Max shook his head. "Pete doesn't go to school here anymore. Pete's dead."

I gasped. "That's horrible! Were you friends with him? What happened?"

"No—you don't understand. Pete died a long time ago. Like, over a hundred years ago. No one knows exactly what happened. All we know is that on his twelfth birthday his body was found in the Fear Street Woods—all shriveled up."

"Eeew." I curled my lip.

"His parents buried him in the Fear Street Cemetery. But the next year, on his birthday, some kids found themselves playing hide-and-seek in the Fear Street Woods—with Pete's ghost. A nasty ghost-kid with a big open wound and blood oozing from his chest."

A light breeze blew a strand of hair across my face. I brushed it away. It seemed strange to be talking about something so creepy on such a beautiful day.

"Since then it's been a town tradition," Max went on. "Every year on Pete's birthday, all the twelve-year-olds go to the woods to play hide-and-seek with him."

"Oh!" I laughed. "You mean, this whole story about Pete is an old legend. And the game is just for fun! Oh! I get it!"

Max coughed a little. "Well, not exactly. If you're twelve, you have to play. Or else."

I giggled. "Or else what?"

"Or else Pete gets angry. He makes bad things happen to everyone in town."

This is a joke. He *must* be teasing me, I thought. "Come on, Max. This is just an old story."

"It is not!" Max insisted. "You don't understand. Pete is a ghost—but he wants to be alive again. So he lives in the body of a twelve-year-old kid. Every year on his birthday, he takes a new body. See, at the hide-and-seek game, Pete is *It*. Whoever he tags—Pete takes over that person's body. He lives in it for a whole year—until the next hide-and-seek game."

I started laughing. "Max, you crack me up! Stop kidding around!" I cried.

Max stared at me as if I were crazy. "I am not kidding! This is all true. Ask anybody!"

"Right. I'd look like an idiot."

Max shrugged. "All right. Don't believe me. It probably doesn't matter this year anyway."

"Why not?"

"Because last year Randy Clay got rid of Pete. She played a trick on him. She sent him back to the cemetery for good." He paused, and added, "I hope so, anyway."

Out of the corner of my eye I spotted Mina at the water fountain. She bent down to take a drink.

Max said, "Most kids think Pete won't show up for

the game this year. But we're going anyway. Just in case . . . Heh-heh." He laughed—a little nervously, I thought.

Mina stood up and leaned toward me and Max. I realized she'd been listening to us.

She moved her pale face close to mine—so close I could feel her breath on my face. Through her veil of black hair she whispered, "I wouldn't be too sure of that. And you're the new girl. Becky Tabor, I'd be careful if I were you! Very careful. Because Pete likes the new kids!"

Chapter FOUR

I felt the blood drain from my face. Suddenly, this story didn't seem so funny.

"What are you talking about?" I demanded.

Mina didn't say another word. She glided away and disappeared in a crowd of kids going back inside the building.

I stared at Max. "What was that all about?"

"Don't listen to her," he said. "She's kind of weird. She used to be pretty normal, but ever since last summer . . . I don't know. She's been strange."

The bell rang. I stood up. "I'd better go to class," I said, grabbing my backpack.

"Me too," Max said. "Listen—don't let Mina scare you. I really think Pete's gone for good. I mean, I don't know for sure . . . but I *think* so."

"But—according to your story—he could still be here?" I asked. "I mean, one of you . . . could be Pete, right?"

"I guess," Max admitted. "Anyone could be Pete."

He jumped at me, baring his teeth and snarling. "Even me!" he growled.

"Aaa!" I squeaked. I jumped back. Max laughed.

"Just kidding," he assured me.

I gave him a good whack on the shoulder so he'd know I didn't think he was funny.

I rode my bike home from school that afternoon. I kept thinking about the story Max had told me. I remembered Darcy saying that people told weird tales about Fear Street.

Was everybody in Shadyside so superstitious? How could they all believe such dumb ghost stories?

I turned my bike down Fear Street and headed toward the cemetery. The hair on the back of my neck stood up again. Just as it had the afternoon before.

Calm down, I told myself. You're as silly as all the other kids in this town! Why should you be nervous just because you're passing by a cemetery?

I stared at the graves as I rode. They *won't* scare me. They *won't* scare me, I chanted to myself.

A dog ran right into my path. "Look out!" I screamed. I tried to swerve my bike away—but my front tire hit the dog!

I slammed on my brakes. Too late! The dog squealed and limped away. I jumped off my bike. I let it crash to the ground as I followed the dog.

"Hey!" I called. "Are you okay?"

The little dog whined. He wouldn't let me come near him.

It's the dog I saw yesterday, I realized. The brown-and-white one. He must be afraid of me now. He must be hurt!

The dog disappeared into the cemetery. "Little dog! Where are you?" I cried. I had to find him. If I could only catch him, I'd take him to the vet and make sure he was okay.

But that meant I'd have to go into the cemetery.

If only I'd watched where I was going! I felt terrible.

Here goes, I thought. I took a deep breath. Then I stepped through the gate. I stared at the rows and rows of old, crumbling tombstones.

I'm not scared, I told myself. I squeezed my hands together to keep them from shaking.

I didn't see the dog anywhere. "Where are you?" I called. I thought I heard a rustle in the weeds.

"Dog? Are you there?"

I moved toward the rustling weeds, deeper into the cemetery. The dog must be behind that grave marker, I thought. I stepped closer.

The dog jumped out from behind the gravestone. He whined as he limped off.

"Come back!" I cried. I tried to follow him, but he had disappeared again. The cemetery was so thick with weeds and bushes, it was easy to lose him.

I stood still and listened. I thought I heard something—whining! The poor thing! I thought.

I hurried toward the whining sound. It stopped. I glanced around.

Ah-ha! I spotted a stubby tail behind a big gravestone.

I crept toward it, hoping the dog wouldn't hear me and run away again.

Almost there . . . closer . . . closer . . .

I reached out toward the grave—but something grabbed my ankle!

I glanced down. Too late.

Whatever it was gripped me tighter.

"Aaaah!" I screamed.

Then it pulled me down to the ground!

Chapter FIVE

Everything started spinning.

I felt myself whirling, down, down, down into the ground. Eerie, hollow voices laughed at me as I fell down a bottomless pit. *Ooo-hoo-hoo!* they laughed. *Ah-ha-ha!*

Wispy white figures darted before my eyes, laughed, and disappeared like smoke. And I kept falling and falling down an endless hole.

At last I stopped falling. I landed on soft ground with a thump. Cautiously, I opened my eyes. Where am I? I wondered.

I sat up and brushed the dirt from my cheek. I was still in the cemetery. A little sunshine filtered through the trees. How long had I been lying there? I couldn't tell.

I glanced around, searching for the dog. There was no sign of him.

I guess he's all right, I thought. I tried to stand up, but I felt a little woozy. My ankle hurt. I must have twisted it and fallen.

Then I realized my head was pounding with a terrible headache too. I must have hit it when I fell. I felt as if I'd just woken up from a nightmare.

I managed to pull myself to my feet. I stumbled out of the cemetery. My bike lay where I'd left it on the side of the road. I picked it up and started for home.

I sped down the street, pedaling as fast as I could. I didn't know why I was riding so fast—I just felt like it. I gritted my teeth and pumped my legs harder.

I wheeled into the driveway at top speed. Martha was standing next to her bike in front of the garage. I squeezed the brakes hard—but not soon enough. I skidded and crashed right into Martha's bike.

Martha glared at me through her little silver-framed glasses. "Hey! What did you do that for?"

I stood in the driveway, breathing hard. What *did* I do that for? I wondered. It wasn't like me to lose control like that.

I picked up Martha's bike. "I'm sorry, Martha," I said. "I didn't mean to." I inspected the bike, adding, "There's a little dent in the fender. But otherwise it looks okay."

Martha snatched the bike from me and studied it herself. "'Haste makes waste,'" she snapped.

"I know, Ben, I know. The bike just . . . got out of control, I guess." I didn't know what else to say. "I'll try to fix it for you."

"'Great talkers, little doers,'" she replied.

"Would you please stop that?" Sometimes I get sick of her Ben Franklin thing.

I went inside to lie down. I felt funny. And I still had a headache.

"Becky, are you feeling all right?" Mom asked.

I nodded. I drew an X in my mashed potatoes with my fork. I wasn't very hungry.

Dad opened the newspaper. "Let's see what Becky's horoscope says."

I felt my temper flaring up. My face grew hot. I narrowed my eyes. Why did Dad always have to read those stupid things at dinner?

"'You may be feeling confused now. Draw on your inner strength, and you will come through a difficult time,'" Dad read. "Are you feeling confused, Becky?"

"No!" I snapped. "Dumb horoscopes!"

I loaded my fork with a big glob of mashed potatoes. I lobbed it at my dad. *Splat!* It hit him on the side of the head.

For a moment, no one said a word. Then Mom broke the silence.

"Becky!" Mom gasped. "What's gotten into you?"

Dad wiped the potatoes from his face. Martha just stared at me with a stunned expression. I stared back. An angry thought raced through my head. *Serves you right!*

I sneered at my family. But my anger disappeared in a second. The sneer faded from my face. My heart raced. I felt scared. Why was I thinking such horrible things?

I dropped my fork and ran to my room.

I threw myself on my bed. My head throbbed like crazy.

I can't believe I threw mashed potatoes at Dad! I thought. I've never done anything like that before.

Why did I do it? I didn't *decide* to do it. I didn't even think about it.

I just did it. It was as if I couldn't stop myself.

I squeezed my aching head with my hands, trying to make it stop hurting.

What's wrong with me? I wondered. What's wrong?

Chapter SIX

I still felt lousy when I woke up the next morning. My stomach growled. My head pounded as if someone were trapped inside it, trying to bash their way out. I dressed and trudged downstairs to breakfast.

"Good morning, honey," Mom chirped. She flipped a stack of pancakes onto a plate and set them in front of me. "You must be hungry. You didn't finish your dinner last night."

I stared at the pancakes. I *was* hungry. And I usually love pancakes. But just then they seemed disgusting to me. The smell made me sick to my stomach.

Martha sat across the table from me. "'Eat to live—don't live to eat,'" she pronounced.

I rolled my eyes and downed a glass of juice. "I've got to get to school, Mom," I said. "See you later."

I grabbed my lunch and hurried out. "Becky!" Mom called after me. "Don't you want some cereal or something?"

"No!" I shouted. I jumped onto my bike and rode to school. Mina was parking her bike just as I pulled up to the rack.

"Hi," I said.

"Hi." She stared at me.

"What are you looking at?" I demanded.

"You—you look strange," she replied.

"Strange? What do you mean?"

"Tired, or something . . ." She shrugged. "I'm sorry. I shouldn't have said anything."

She turned and walked away.

What a weird girl, I thought. I locked my bike and went inside.

I managed to gulp down my sandwich at lunch. I started to feel a little bit better. After lunch I sat with Darcy and some other kids in the hallway.

"My mom doesn't want me to play hide-and-seek this year," a girl named Laura announced. "I told her, 'Mom—I have to! Haven't you heard what happens if we don't? Pete terrorizes everybody from his grave. People get sick. Dogs and cats start mysteriously disappearing. Kids wake up to find their faces rotting off their heads!'"

"I think it's safe to play this year," Darcy declared. "Randy got rid of him, right?"

"But he could come back," said a boy named Jeff. "What if he shows up somehow? What if one of us is Pete now—only we don't know it?"

"Jeff, are you Pete?" Darcy asked.

"N-no!" Jeff stammered.

"But how can we be sure?" Darcy went on. "If you *were* Pete, you'd lie about it, wouldn't you?"

"*I'm* not Pete!" Jeff insisted. "Maybe *you* are!"

"Oh, puh-leez!" Darcy huffed. She studied her fingernails. "Yeah, *I'm* Pete. Really."

"Pete's ghost is so gross," Laura put in. "I heard he has a big, bloody wound in the middle of his chest. His teeth are all black and rotten. And he stinks!"

"Come on. You don't really believe those stories, do you?" I asked.

Jeff laughed and jerked his thumb at me. "The new kid."

"What does *that* mean?" I demanded.

Now Laura and Darcy laughed too. "Everyone knows that Pete likes to go after new kids," Darcy explained.

"Whatever. This Pete stuff is ridiculous," I said. I leaned against a locker, hugging my knees. I watched the kids pass by.

Down the hall, I saw Max walking toward us, his

arms loaded with books. "Hey, guys," he called.

He stepped near me. Suddenly, I felt my leg twitch. It was as though it wanted to shoot out in front of me. Right into Max's path.

No! I thought. No! Stop twitching!

But I couldn't stop it. Just as Max passed me, my leg kicked out.

His foot caught beneath my leg.

And he went flying.

Chapter SEVEN

"Whoa!"

Max crashed to the floor. His books scattered everywhere.

I quickly yanked my leg back. The other kids started laughing.

Max sat up, red-faced, and turned to me. "What did you do that for?" he asked angrily.

I squeezed my leg, but it wasn't twitching anymore. "I—I don't know," I stammered. "S-s-sorry."

"Sorry! You did that on purpose!"

The others laughed even harder now. I didn't know what to say.

I didn't know why my leg kicked out like that. I didn't mean to do it. I didn't *want* to do it. My leg did it—by itself.

"Max, I couldn't help it. It was like a twitch or something. It just—happened."

Max gathered his books and stalked away. I spotted Mina leaning against the wall across the hall. She was staring at me again—staring hard.

I glanced away, hugging my knees to my chest.

Thump, thump, thump went the ache inside my head.

"Aren't you going to read us our horoscopes tonight, Dad?" Martha asked at dinner that night.

"I don't dare." Dad glanced at me. "I'm afraid I'll get a forkful of food thrown at me."

"I'm really sorry about that, Dad," I said, gazing down at my plate. What else could I say? I had no idea why I did it. I seemed to be losing control of myself lately.

"That's all right," Dad said. "We're all allowed to be a little crazy once in a while."

I picked up my knife and sawed at my steak. At last, I thought. Something I felt like eating. I cut away the meat and picked up the bone. I gnawed on the fat.

Martha raised her fork in the air. "'We may give advice, but we do not inspire conduct.'"

"Whatever that means," I snapped.

"Now, *Martha* is another story," Dad teased. "She's a little crazy *all* the time."

"Really, Martha," Mom said. "I'm glad you admire Benjamin Franklin. But you're *not* the reincarnation of him. I'm your mother. I'd know it if you were."

"Mom, I *am* Ben Franklin. And by the way, I need another bottle of ink for my quill pen. I can't do my homework without it."

"I want to see the real Martha," Dad insisted. "I know she's in there somewhere."

I listened quietly, gnawing on my steak bones.

"Close your eyes, Martha," Dad went on. "Reach deep inside. Your real self is in there. Now call her up." Dad spoke in a low, spooky voice. "Say, 'Martha, Martha, Martha.'"

Martha closed her eyes. "Martha, Martha, Martha," she repeated.

She opened her eyes. "Well?" Mom said.

"'He who lies with the dogs, riseth with fleas,'" Martha declared.

Dad dropped his head into his hands. "That's it. I give up!"

I reached across the table for Mom's steak bone. "You want that?" I mumbled.

"No," Mom replied, staring as I snatched it off her plate. "But why should you?"

"I don't know." I sucked on the bone. "I just like it."

"Aren't you going to eat your meat?" Mom demanded.

"I like the fat," I said. "And the bones."

"Ugh!" Dad wailed. "That's gross."

I glanced at Martha. She was looking at me strangely.

"Stop staring at me!" I cried. "I don't need this!" I pushed away from the table and stomped upstairs.

"Becky, wait!" Martha cried. She chased after me, stopping me at the top of the stairs.

"What do you want?" I huffed.

"Well—remember you asked me about that game that all the twelve-year-olds play?" she said. "I found out a little more about it. About Pete."

That pounding in my head started again.

"Who cares?" I snapped. "All I ever hear about is Pete, Pete, Pete! Why don't you go soak your stupid little Ben Franklin head!"

"Becky!" Mom called. "Don't talk to your sister like that!"

I stormed off to my room. I reached out to slam the door—and stopped.

A lump caught in my throat.

I took one look at the floor—and screamed!

Chapter EIGHT

My old Raggedy Ann doll lay on the floor. A big gash was ripped right through her stomach. All her stuffing had been pulled out!

"No!" I screamed. "Who did this?"

I kneeled on the floor and picked up my doll. I cradled her in my arms. I knew it was only a stuffed toy, but . . . it felt as if she had been murdered. Who would do something so mean?

"Martha!" I shouted. "Did you do this?"

Martha appeared in the doorway. "Your doll," she gasped. "No, I didn't do it."

"You must have!" I insisted. "Who else would?"

She shrugged. "Maybe *you* did it, Becky."

"Give me a break, Martha," I said. "Why would I rip up my own doll?"

"I don't know. But I've been meaning to talk to you about something. Last night—you threw a fit in your room. Don't you remember?"

"What are you talking about?" I demanded.

"I heard you last night. It sounded like you were going crazy! You probably ripped up your doll then. You were kind of growling—like an animal!"

My head began to spin.

What was Martha talking about? I didn't remember throwing a fit, or tearing up my doll. I didn't remember anything like that!

But it wasn't like Martha to lie about it. The Ben Franklin in her kept her blunt and honest.

I collapsed on my bed, clutching my dizzy, pounding head. I'm so confused! I thought desperately. What's happening to me? How could I have done something so strange—and not remember it?

"Becky?" Martha crept farther into the room. "Becky—are you okay?"

"No," I moaned. "I'm not."

"Hey, Becky, do you want your apple?" Darcy and I sat together in the cafeteria. She was eyeing my untouched lunch.

"Here." I passed her the apple. "You eat it."

She grabbed the apple and took a huge bite out of it.

"Aren't you going to eat *anything*?" she asked.

I shook my head. "I'm really hungry. But every-thing smells so gross in here. It makes me feel kind of sick."

Darcy studied my face as she munched on the apple. "You don't look well," she commented. She passed the apple back to me. "On second thought, you better eat this."

The white part of the apple was already brown-ing. I grimaced. "No thanks. I think I'll go outside and get some fresh air."

I practically ran from the stinky cafeteria and out to the playground. I didn't think about where I was going. My legs carried me by themselves. I passed the swings, passed the basketball nets. I hurried out to the edge of the playing field and sat on the grass.

The earth was soft and damp beneath me. It had rained that morning. My hand pawed at the dirt. I found myself clawing through the soil, digging. I was looking for something, but I didn't know what.

I dug deeper. My fingernails filled with dirt. Then I stopped. I'd found what I was looking for.

A worm.

I'm so hungry, I thought.

I picked up the worm. I watched it wiggle between my fingers.

Wait, I thought. Someone's watching me. I can feel it.

I glanced up. Mina stood a few yards away. She

stared at me intently. Her eyes were big and round, like a hypnotist's. She didn't blink. She just stared— as if she were trying to read my mind. Or trying to send me a telepathic message.

A voice in my head said, "Eat it! Eat it!"

I tilted my head back. I dangled the worm over my open mouth.

Then I dropped it in—and chewed.

Chapter NINE

The worm wiggled against my tongue. I bit down on it. It got all mushy.

Then I swallowed it.

"Uhhh!" I groaned. "Disgusting!" I tried to spit it out. But it was too late.

I curled up on the grass, clutching my stomach. Why did I do that? That is the grossest thing I have ever done in my life!

The earthy taste stayed on my tongue. I kept saying, "Blech! Blech!"

I didn't want to eat a worm. But I couldn't stop myself!

Okay, calm down. I told myself. There's got to be a logical, rational reason for this.

I thought for a moment. I haven't been feeling

right lately. I need to eat more vegetables. Maybe I'm missing something in my diet—some kind of vitamin or mineral.

Yeah, that's it! That might explain why I have these weird food cravings. And why this headache won't go away.

I sat up—and found Mina standing beside me. I hadn't heard her coming.

Her big eyes seemed to burn right through me. "I saw you," she whispered. "You didn't want to eat it, did you? But you did it anyway. I knew you would."

My mouth fell open. I didn't know what to say. She ran away across the field.

Her words echoed in my head. I still felt her her eyes burning into me.

Could she—could she be—I wondered.

No. I shook the thought from my mind. It was too weird. Too impossible.

I stared at the hole I'd dug in the ground. Then at my hand, covered with brown dirt. I felt as if I couldn't control my hand, I remembered. As if, somehow, someone was *forcing* me to dig up—and eat—a worm.

And there stood Mina. Staring at me while I did it. In fact, she was *always* staring at me.

I wiggled my head, trying to shake some sense into it. Get yourself together! I scolded myself. This headache is making you crazy!

I didn't know what was going on with me. But I

knew one thing for sure. Mina was a *really* weird girl.

Instead of going back to class, I decided to head home. It was no use staying in school. I couldn't think clearly anyway. I just wanted to lie down.

I glanced up at the sky. The sun was shining. I began the long walk home.

I turned onto Fear Street and passed the Fear Street Woods. I thought about the hide-and-seek game. June tenth. It was coming soon.

Nobody seems worried about it, I thought. It might be fun.

But even in the sunshine, the woods sure looked spooky.

I stopped for a second to shift my backpack to my left arm. I thought I heard something.

Footsteps!

I whirled around. No one was there.

I stared into the woods. I didn't see anyone.

It's probably nothing, I told myself. I must have heard the pounding in my own head.

I started walking again. Another noise came from behind me. This time I *knew* I'd heard something. A swishing sound—the sound of dead leaves rustling.

I wheeled around again. The noise stopped. But this time I saw something.

Some*one*.

Crouched in the shadow of a tree—watching me!

Chapter TEN

Someone was following me! Spying on me!

"Stop!" I cried. I ran into the woods to see who was there. The figure saw me coming. Whoever it was withdrew into the shadows—and ran for cover.

"Wait!" I shouted. I chased the figure as fast as I could. But it was too fast for me.

I stopped. I could hear the spy far ahead of me, running away. But I couldn't see who it was.

I leaned forward to catch my breath. I was shaking.

Why would someone follow me? I thought. Why was someone hiding in the Fear Street Woods?

I continued walking home, but kept glancing nervously over my shoulder. Was anyone following me?

I didn't see anyone.

But still—I definitely didn't feel as if I were alone.

I sat up in bed and punched my pillow. It felt like a rock. I laid my head down on it again. I rolled over.

This stupid headache! I groaned. When will it leave me alone?

It was almost midnight. I was tossing and turning, trying to fall asleep. But my head kept pounding. My arms and legs felt strangely restless. As if they were itching to go out for a run.

I closed my eyes. I watched colors swirl behind my eyelids. I began to feel that gentle rocking feeling. Ah, I thought. I'm falling asleep at last . . .

Then something woke me. I felt cold. With my eyes still shut, I groped for my covers.

Couldn't find them. Where were they?

I reached back and touched my headboard. But I didn't feel its warm, smooth wood. Instead it felt rough and cold like—like—

Oh, no.

Like stone.

I opened my eyes. I turned—and screamed.

HERE LIES ANNA JOHNSON, I read.

In place of my headboard, I stared at a tombstone!

I jumped to my feet. "No! No!" I cried.

I was in the Fear Street Cemetery. And I'd been sleeping on top of somebody's grave!

"What am I doing here?" I shrieked. "How did I get here?"

I broke out in a cold sweat. I remembered falling asleep at home, in my own bed. How did I end up in a graveyard in the middle of the night?

My mind raced, but I couldn't think clearly. Could someone have kidnapped me? I wondered. Did I sleepwalk over here?

Then I got a creepy feeling. A familiar feeling. The feeling that someone was watching me.

"Who's out there?" I shouted. "I know you're spying on me. Who are you?"

No one answered.

I peered through the darkness. A shaft of moonlight glowed on a nearby graveyard plot.

Something moved. Something shiny and black. Behind a tombstone a few feet away.

"Who's there?" I called again.

Silence.

I crept toward the tombstone. A small, round black thing jutted up above it.

Black hair shone in the moonlight. Someone's head!

I rushed to the stone and peeked behind it.

"Mina!" I gasped.

She stared at me with her huge, hypnotic blue eyes.

"Mina—why are you spying on me?" I demanded.

"The game . . ." she murmured.

I grabbed her by the shoulders and shook her. "What about the game?" I asked.

"The game," she repeated. "You're *It*."

She slipped out of my grip and disappeared into the shadows.

I watched her vanish. A shiver raced through my body. I glanced down. No wonder! I was wearing only my nightgown, and my feet were bare.

A cloud covered the moon, making the darkness thicker than ever. I cowered behind a tree. What was Mina talking about? Why did she say *I* was It? We weren't playing tag.

And why was she hiding in the cemetery? Did she bring me there somehow?

Awoooo! A soft howl met my ears.

What was that?

Awoooo!

Only the wind in the trees, I told myself. It's only the wind.

But I didn't want to hang around to make sure. I hurried across the damp grass, out to the street. I wanted to be home, safe in my bed—and *stay* there.

I ran out of the cemetery and down Fear Street. Bits of gravel dug into my feet, but I didn't care.

Mina's voice echoed in my head. "The game," she murmured. "The game . . ."

I gasped.

A terrible thought sprang into my head.

I remembered what I heard kids at school say about Pete. "Pete hangs out in the cemetery," they'd said. "Pete likes to go after new kids."

New kids. Like me!

"Maybe one of us is Pete now," Jeff had said.

I froze. A prickle of fear crept up my spine.

Maybe someone at school *was* Pete.

Someone weird. Someone creepy.

Someone like Mina!

Chapter ELEVEN

"**B**ecky, are you okay?"

Darcy peered into my face. I was trudging down the hall at school, feeling like a zombie. I noticed people staring at me, giving me funny looks, but I didn't know why. All I knew was that I felt exhausted.

"Why?" I asked. "Don't I *look* okay?"

"Well, your eyes are all puffy and red," Darcy said. "You look like you were up all night or something."

"Well, I wasn't," I replied quickly. There was no way I was letting anyone know about my little trip to the cemetery last night.

Way down the hall, I spotted Max loping along with his usual armload of books. I wanted to talk to him. I *had* to talk to him. About Mina—and Pete.

"I'll see you later, Darcy," I said. I took off down the hall after Max, following his big mess of curly brown hair.

I dodged left and right, around big groups of students. Suddenly, Max's head disappeared around a corner. I put on some speed. I couldn't lose him in the crowd!

I rounded the corner, and screeched to a stop. Max stood right in front of me. "Hey!" I yelled. "I have to talk to you!"

I must have startled him.

"Yaa!" he yelled. He juggled his armload of books, then dropped them all over the floor. Again.

"Oops," I said. "Sorry."

"What do you want?" he grumbled, picking up a huge textbook.

I stooped down to help him. "Max—I really am sorry about this. And I'm really, *really* sorry I tripped you the other day," I insisted. "I didn't mean to—I swear!"

"It's okay," he said. "I believe you. You don't seem like a girl who trips people as a hobby." He gave me a smile.

I glanced around the hall, checking to see if anyone was listening. I had to find out if Mina was Pete. And I had to find out now.

"Want to go sit outside for a minute?" I suggested. "I need to ask you something."

Max shrugged and nodded. "Sure." We headed out into the sunshine and sat on a bench.

"What's up?" Max asked.

"Well—you know, that *game* is coming up," I hinted. "And I'm new, and I don't really know much about it. Can you tell me more about Pete? You seem to know a lot about him."

"I know only what my older brother told me," Max admitted. "His friend David was tagged in the game a couple of years ago. Pete took over his body for an entire year."

"What happened? What did Pete do with David's body?" I asked, anxious.

"David acted weird the whole year. You could tell he wasn't himself."

I remembered something Max told me the first day I met Mina: *She used to be pretty normal, but ever since last summer . . . she's been strange.*

"Pete made David do mean things," Max went on. "Gross things."

"Like what?"

"Like . . ." Max thought for a minute. "Well, my brother Joe was his best friend. But sometimes David would punch him—for no reason! Pete was always making David trip people, slap people . . . and break things. David collected old records—he was really into it. But Pete made him smash them up—every single one of them."

As I listened, a little knot formed in my stomach. It slowly tightened with every word Max said.

Pete makes you hurt people for no reason, and break your own things, I thought.

I felt ill. So far that didn't sound like Mina.

"Pete used to keep David up all night. Sometimes David found himself in the cemetery—in the middle of the night! He had no idea how he got there."

The knot in my stomach turned to a rock. My heart raced. Stop! I thought. I don't want to hear any more!

"Pete even made David eat gross things," Max said. "Like dirt. And worms!"

My heart raced so fast, I could hardly breathe. Everything Max was saying . . .

I didn't want to think about it. I pressed my hands against my eyes until I saw stars.

No, I thought. No! It's too horrible!

It can't be!

Waking up in the cemetery. Eating worms!

Mina didn't do any of those things.

I did!

My throat went completely dry as the awful thought hit me

What if *I'm* Pete?

I lay awake again that night, my head throbbing. It didn't matter how tired I was—I just couldn't sleep. I was too terrified to sleep.

Max's words kept echoing in my head. *He woke up in the cemetery. He ate worms.*

The weird things Pete made people do sounded too much—way too much—like the weird things *I'd* been doing lately.

I didn't want to believe it. My mind screamed against the idea, fighting it. I was just tired. Or stressed out. Or not eating right.

It couldn't be true. It *wasn't* true!

I couldn't be Pete. I was Becky! Becky!

I remembered what my parents had said to Martha at dinner one night. "Call up your true self," they had said. "Close your eyes and say 'Martha, Martha, Martha.'"

I'm going to do it, I decided. Maybe it will make me feel better. I'm a strong-willed person. I'll call up my inner self—and all this silliness will stop.

I closed my eyes and took a deep breath.

"Becky, Becky, Becky," I whispered.

I waited. I didn't feel anything.

I wasn't sure what I was supposed to feel. But I imagined a surge of strength, or a clear, calm feeling.

I'll try it again, I thought.

This time I said my name a little louder: "Becky, Becky, Becky."

Nothing happened. I started feeling nervous.

Where was my inner strength? My inner self? It was as if Becky weren't there at all!

One more time, I vowed. It's going to work this time.

This time I'm going to get an answer.

"Becky, Becky, Becky!"

Something stirred inside me. I felt a voice bubble up from somewhere deep. It shot through my body and up to my brain.

I got my answer.

The voice said, "*Pete*."

Chapter TWELVE

A lump caught in my throat. My eyes flew open.

"Who said that?" I demanded.

The voice spoke again, inside my head. It wasn't my voice. Not at all.

"Haven't you figured it out yet?" the harsh and raspy voice uttered. "I'm Pete!"

"No!" I whispered. "No!"

My body trembled with fear. I wanted to cry. How could this happen to me?

"That's right—it's me!" Pete laughed hoarsely. "The famous Pete you've heard so much about. I'm using your body for a while. You don't mind, do you?"

I lay there, frozen. Shaking. Listening. I couldn't believe it! I was having a conversation with someone else—inside my own head!

"I'm making you do what *I* want you to do," Pete rasped. "*I'm* in control now. Like that game, *Simon Says*. Only I call it Pete Says. And what Pete says, *you do*!"

"Get out of me!" I cried. "Get out—now!"

Pete's laughter seemed to bounce off the inside of my skull. I clutched my head and pounded it on the pillow, trying to shake him out.

He only laughed harder.

"You can't get rid of me," he boasted. "Just relax. You're kind of lucky. You won't have to put up with me for long."

"But everyone said you were gone," I wailed. "They said you were trapped in the cemetery! How did you get out? How did you get inside me?"

"Easy," Pete explained. "One day a dog came sniffing through the graveyard. I snatched him and took over his body. As long as I was inside a live body, I could leave the graveyard whenever I wanted!"

"A dog—" I gasped. "You mean—that dog I hit with my bike?"

"That's the one. He's a smelly old thing. I hated being inside him. I just needed him to get out so I could find a kid to take over. Nobody can keep me trapped in my grave for a whole year!"

"But I still don't understand—" I started to say.

"I hope you're not a complete moron," Pete interrupted. "I'll need access to your brain—so it better be a good one."

"But—"

"Kids don't go skipping through the graveyard every day, you know!" Pete snapped. "I needed to lure one in. So I went out as a dog and threw myself under the wheel of your bike. I knew you'd follow me into the graveyard if you thought I was hurt. Once I had you there, I left the dog's body and took over yours."

I felt dizzy. It all made sense now. Every weird thing that had happened since I moved to Shadyside—it all had to do with Pete.

"Ha-ha-ha-ha!" Pete snickered. "The look on your face that day! That was hilarious. You were really worried about that stupid dog!"

"Get out of me!" I shrieked. "I hate you!"

"Sorry. Can't do that," Pete replied. "No. Not until my birthday. You're coming to my party in the woods, aren't you? Oh, that's right—you have no choice!" He laughed again.

"I need to get to the woods for the hide-and-seek game," he went on. "And I can't do that without your body. But don't worry. I'll tag someone else at the game, and take *their* body. Until then, Becky— I'm you, and you're me.

"And there's nothing you can do about it."

Chapter THIRTEEN

No! I thought. There must be something I can do to get rid of Pete!

I was sitting at the back of the room in algebra, staring out the window.

I've got to get Pete out of my body! There must be a way.

"Who has the answer for problem three—Becky?"

I glanced up. Mr. Hume, my algebra teacher, was calling on me. But not because I'd raised my hand. I never raised my hand in class lately.

After all, my body was *possessed by a ghost*! That made school pretty much a joke. Who cared about tests and reports? I had more important things to worry about.

"Sorry, Mr. Hume," I mumbled. "I didn't do my homework last night."

Mr. Hume frowned. "See me after class, Becky."

The bell rang a few minutes later. I didn't hang around to see Mr. Hume after class. I dashed right out of there.

"Becky!" he called after me. "Get back here! I'm giving you detention!"

"So what?" I grumbled. "I've got bigger problems."

I marched through the lunch line, grabbing a plate of meat loaf and mashed potatoes without thinking much about it.

I turned my head quickly and caught Mina staring at me. She looked quickly away.

What is she hanging around me for? I wondered. I noticed she carried a brown paper lunch bag in her hand. She was following me through the cafeteria line—but she wasn't buying any food.

I carried my tray into the lunchroom. Mina settled at a table, eyeing me.

Look at all these kids, I thought—eating their lunches as if nothing were wrong.

They all think Pete's gone.

But he's back now—and he's *me*! He's going to tag one of them on his birthday! It'll be so easy for him this year. They all think they're safe.

I've got to warn them—before it's too late!

I grabbed my tray and sat down next to Max and

Darcy. I'm going to tell them, I decided. Then maybe they can warn the others. . . .

"Hey, Becky," Max said. "Don't you usually bring your own lunch to school?"

"I forgot it today," I explained. "Listen—"

"Becky, you look worse every day," Darcy interrupted. She was staring at my eyes. "Are you sick or something?"

"Not exactly," I said. "Listen, you guys. I've got something important to tell you. About the hide-and-seek game—be careful—"

I thought I heard a voice in my head rasp out, "Oh, no, you don't!"

And then—

Splat!

Suddenly I found my face smashed down into my mashed potatoes!

Chapter FOURTEEN

I lifted my head off my tray, sputtering. I could feel warm goop sticking to my cheeks, my forehead, my nose, and my hair.

How did that happen? I wondered.

Max and Darcy burst out laughing. Everybody around us started laughing too.

My face was *covered* with food. I wiped a blob of mashed potatoes from my eyes. Ketchup oozed down my shirt like blood.

"That was the funniest thing I've ever seen!" Darcy cried, gasping with laughter. "Becky—you should see your face!"

Pete! I thought furiously. He shoved my face in my food to keep me from warning them! And they think it's funny!

"Listen to me!" I shrieked. "It's not funny!"

Everybody howled with laughter, louder than ever.

"I mean it! The hide-and-seek game—you've got to—"

Pete smashed my face down again! Kids were screaming with delight. They were practically rolling on the floor.

I tried to wipe off my face as best as I could.

"I didn't know you were so funny!" Max managed to get out through his laughter.

I sighed. They'd never listen to me now. They all thought it was a big joke.

I can't believe this, I thought. Pete is really controlling my body. He won't even let me talk!

And then, suddenly . . .

My legs straightened. I stood up. I turned away from the table. My legs carried me out of the cafeteria.

I wasn't controlling my body at all. Pete was.

No! I protested. *I won't go to the basement! You can't make me*!

I tried to stop walking. I summoned all my strength to plant my feet on the floor. But my feet wouldn't do what I told them to do. They kept going.

Stop! I shouted to myself.

I grabbed the door of the cafeteria. My legs kept walking, pulling me out. I clung to the door frame.

What do you want? I demanded silently. What are you going to make me do?

Behind me, I heard the whole cafeteria screaming with laughter. Everyone was watching me. I had food in my hair and all over my face, and my body was totally out of control.

If only they knew how terrified I was!

I gripped the door frame in a panic. He's going to do something horrible! I thought. I won't go!

But Pete had other ideas. He made my fingers peel off the frame, one by one.

Out into the hall and down the stairs. No, no, no! I chanted in my head. Why are you making me go to the basement?

I tried to fight him every step of the way. But I couldn't stop myself.

I sneaked to the basement. It was dark down there. No one was around.

My feet shuffled down the hall. My hand reached for a doorknob. I strained to hold it back. But my hand wouldn't obey me. It turned the knob and opened the door.

The boiler room. A little light trickled in from a small, grimy window near the ceiling.

I grabbed the door frame. But Pete pushed me inside. Something brushed against my face. I swiped at it.

Ugh! Cobwebs!

The door slammed shut behind me. I heard squeaking and scurrying.

My stomach turned. Rats!

I scanned the room. The boiler loomed like a metal monster, dusty and still. Cobwebs clung to the corners. Through the shadows I spotted a huge rat.

Pete made my body move more quickly than it ever had before. I darted to the corner and tried to catch the rat by the tail!

Missed!

Thank goodness, I thought, shuddering. I don't *want* to catch a rat!

Then I saw something against the wall. A mouse-trap.

I crept up to the trap.

Gross! Inside lay a dead mouse.

No! I screamed in my head. I struggled with all my might to stay away from that mouse.

Still my hands picked up the trap. Opened the hinge. My fingers grabbed the mouse by its tail.

I wanted to throw up. I couldn't believe the disgusting thing I was doing.

I dropped the mouse into my pocket. Then I sneaked back upstairs to the cafeteria.

No, Pete, no! What are you doing? What are you making me do with the dead mouse?

Pete didn't answer. But his bitter laughter rang in my ears. *Ha-ha-ha.*

My feet carried me back to the table. I sat down next to Darcy.

She started giggling again at the sight of me. "Where did you go? I thought you went to the bathroom to clean up—but you've still got gunk in your hair."

I tried to speak. "I went down—umph!" My own hand stuffed potatoes into my mouth!

Darcy bent over laughing. Her eyes closed for a few seconds.

My hand reached into my pocket and plucked out the mouse. I struggled to stop my hand. But there was nothing I could do but watch, powerless.

Totally powerless, as Pete made me slip the mouse into Darcy's tuna sandwich.

The sight of the mouse on her food made me sick again. But I quickly pulled my hand away. When Darcy looked at me again, Pete forced my lips up into a smile.

She reached for her sandwich. . . .

I've got to warn her! I thought. I can't let her eat that!

"Darcy!" I cried. But as soon as I opened my mouth, Pete stuffed it with food!

"What?" Darcy asked.

"Mmmfff mmmfff!" I tried to talk, but I couldn't get the words out.

"Becky, quit clowning around. You're getting a little weird."

Darcy picked up her sandwich. She opened her mouth. She let her perfect white teeth sink in.

Chapter FIFTEEN

I winced as she bit into the sandwich. She chewed.

I waited for her scream of horror. But it didn't come. She set the sandwich down again.

She didn't get the mouse that time, I realized with relief. Maybe there's still time to stop her, somehow. . . .

"Hey, Darcy," Max said. "What's that?" He pointed at Darcy's sandwich.

"What's what?" Darcy asked.

"That brown thing."

Thank goodness! Someone noticed! I thought.

"It looks like a mouse tail," Max said.

Darcy lifted up the top slice of bread. The dead mouse lay on top of a bed of tuna.

"Aaaaaaaaaaaaaaah!" Darcy's scream ripped

through the cafeteria. "A mouse! A mouse in my sandwich! Aaaaaaah!

"How did it get there?" she demanded. "Who put that mouse there?"

I wanted to throw up, or cry, or run away and hide. I didn't feel like laughing at all—I swear I didn't.

But Pete did. He lifted the corners of my lips. He opened my mouth and made me laugh.

I laughed harder and harder. I couldn't stop. I felt the eyes of everyone in the cafteria. They all stared at me, burning holes through my head. They hated me. I could feel it.

I glimpsed Mina across the room, with her weird, hypnotic gaze.

But I couldn't stop laughing. To look at me, you would have thought I was the happiest girl in the world.

Or the craziest.

Darcy glared at me and stormed out of the room. I wanted to stop her. I wanted to run after her and explain. But all I could do was laugh.

"Becky, what's the matter with you?" Max asked. "You used to be so nice."

I heard kids whispering all around me. "Look at her—what a weirdo!"

"That's the grossest thing I've ever seen! She must be sick."

"She better be playing in the hide-and-seek game. If Pete shows up, I hope he tags her. Even Pete would be better than Becky!"

If you only knew, I thought miserably. I already *am* Pete! But he won't let me tell anyone!

I tore out of the cafeteria and ran home. I didn't know if Pete was making me do it—or if I was doing it myself. I didn't care. I just wanted to get away.

I ran past the Fear Street Woods, past the cemetery, my mind racing. Pete is taking more and more power over me, I worried. I have less control over my body every day!

Soon I'll be acting like Pete all the time, I realized. He's ruining my life!

On June tenth, he'll ruin someone else's life too.

June tenth is only three days away.

I've got to stop him! I've got to get rid of Pete— and I don't have much time. I've got to do it before the game.

But how?

Chapter SIXTEEN

"**H**ey, Beck. Aren't you home kind of early?"

Martha strolled in from school later that afternoon. I sat slumped on the couch, staring at cartoons on TV. Every time I tried to change the channel, Pete made my hand drop the remote control.

Martha! I was glad to see her. Maybe she could help me somehow.

I wanted to cry out to her, Martha! Help!

I opened my mouth to speak. But what came out was not what I meant to say.

"Mind your own business, twerp. Go get me some chips."

My hand flew to my throat. My vocal cords felt tight.

Oh, no, I thought. He's not just stopping me from

talking. Now he's controlling what I say! And he's getting stronger by the hour!

Martha stared at me. She looked hurt. We usually get along pretty well.

"Get your own chips," she snapped.

"*You* get them," I croaked. "Or I'll shove your head in the toilet!"

Martha's jaw dropped. She's smart. She knew something strange was happening.

"Becky, what's wrong with you?" she demanded. "You've been acting weirder and weirder every day."

Good, Martha! I thought. If only I could tell her!

"Shut up, dogface. Can't you see I'm watching TV?"

Martha frowned and quoted, "'Tart words make no friends—more flies are taken with a drop of honey than a ton of vinegar.'"

"Blah blah blah," I replied.

Martha stormed into the kitchen.

My eyes turned back to the TV. I felt my vocal cords relax. Pete must have been caught up watching cartoons.

Maybe Pete will let *me* talk now, I thought, touching my throat. As long as I don't give him away.

I decided to test it. "Martha—bring me some chips, please," I called.

It worked! Pete let me talk—he just wouldn't let me talk about *him*.

Martha brought the chips and set them on the coffee table. She sat down beside me on the couch.

"'God helps him who helps himself,'" she quoted. "But I brought you your chips just this once." She dug into the bowl and started munching.

If only I could talk to her, I thought. Without Pete knowing what I'm saying. She knows about ghosts and supernatural stuff. She might know a way to get Pete out of my body!

"'An apple a day keeps the doctor away,'" Martha said. "But I'd rather eat chips."

Ben Franklin again, I thought. Then an idea struck me.

That's it! The code!

For awhile, Martha and I used the Ben Franklin code all the time. Our parents never knew what we were saying. Maybe Pete wouldn't know either!

I had to be careful not to give myself away. "Martha—" I began. "Um—" I tried to remember the code. "Um—'The tongue ever turns to the aching tooth.'"

That meant "Something is bothering me—a lot."

Martha's eyes widened. Don't give me away, I silently begged her.

She didn't. But she looked puzzled.

"'Fish and visitors smell after three days,'" I went on.

That meant that Aunt Abigail—we both hated

her—was visiting. I was hoping Martha would get my hint—that someone unwanted was around.

"Aunt Abigail?" she asked.

I shook my head. "Not Aunt Abigail," I muttered. I racked my brain, trying to come up with something else I could say in code.

"Becky, are you trying to tell me something?"

No! I thought. Don't give me away!

Had Pete heard her? Was he on to me?

I sat perfectly still for a second. I waited to see if he'd stop me from talking.

I stared at the TV. A cartoon mouse set a trap for a cat. Pete didn't stir.

It's okay, I told myself. Keep trying.

"'In youth the spirit is exterior, Martha,'" I said. "*My* spirit is *interior*."

"You mean you feel old?" she asked.

"No." I tried to keep my voice steady and calm. Please, I begged silently. This has to work! "I mean, my *spirit*. It's—um—inside me."

Martha stared at me, her forehead creased in puzzlement.

Then, suddenly, all the color drained from her face. Her eyes grew completely round. Her mouth fell open.

She gets it! I thought. She understands!

"You—" she began.

I glared frantically at her. Don't say anything! I

screamed silently. Don't give it away to Pete!

Martha's mouth snapped shut. She sat there for a few seconds, gazing at me with an incredibly shocked look on her face.

Then her mind began to work again. I could practically see the wheels turning.

I would never tell her this to her face. But Martha is one of the smartest people I know. I'm really lucky to have her as a little sister.

"You—uh—you mean you're not quite yourself, huh, Beck?" she asked.

I winced. Would Pete know what Martha meant?

"'Forewarned is forearmed,'" she added. That meant "Get ready. I've got a plan."

She left the room. I stayed in front of the TV. Cartoons seemed to calm Pete down.

I wondered what Martha was up to. But I didn't dare ask. Or Pete might figure out that something was up.

After half an hour, I became more nervous. What if Martha couldn't think of anything to do? What if Pete really was unbeatable? I'd be stuck dong his evil bidding. Until he found another body to live in.

Just then Martha reappeared. "Becky," she said in a strangely chirpy voice, "I have a cool surprise for you."

I felt Pete stir inside me. My throat tightened up again.

"What is it?" Pete made me ask.

"Follow me," Martha said. "You'll love it."

Pete must have been curious. I stood up. Martha led me to the bathroom. She shut the door behind us.

The bathroom smelled like perfume. Martha had filled the tub with herbs, oils, and magic stuff.

"Get in," Martha ordered.

Pete made me dive for the door. Martha blocked it.

"Get in," she repeated. She gave me a rough shove into the tub.

I splashed into the water—clothes and all.

Then she reached behind the toilet and pulled out something she must have been hiding. A book!

I read the title engraved in big, gold letters on the spine: *The Magic of Colonial Times*.

"I found a spell in this book," Martha said. "It's supposed to suck spirits out of the body."

"NOOOOOO! Stupid girl! Don't you know who I am?" the ghost inside me roared. "I am Pete! And you are no match for me! You'll never get me out of here!"

Martha shook a little. Stay calm, Martha, I prayed. And please let this work!

"Try to get rid of me," Pete dared her. "Go ahead."

At least he's not trying to escape, I thought. I squirmed in the tub. My clothes were getting oily.

Martha dipped her fingers in the tub and dotted oil on my forehead.

"One body, one spirit," Martha chanted. "Unwanted spirit—leave! Teka-tika-tok!"

She took a handful of herbs and dumped them on my head.

"Calling Pete! Calling Pete!" she cried. "Leave Becky's body. Leave it now! Out! Out! Out!"

I felt something. My body started trembling. Then shaking. Harder and harder.

I got excited. Something was definitely happening!

"Becky!" Martha cried. "Do you feel something?"

My body shook so hard, my eyes blurred.

"It's working!" Martha shouted. "I don't believe it!"

I felt something pushing me. It started in my stomach. It pushed up, higher, through my chest. It pushed up through my throat, into my head. It pushed against my brain.

I couldn't make anything out. I was shaking so fast! Streaks of light and colors flashed before my eyes.

It's working! I thought. I think it's working!

Chapter SEVENTEEN

I heard a rush of noise, like wind in a tunnel. I felt one final, strong push.

Then everything stopped.

I stopped shaking. Everything was quiet and still.

I felt funny. All light and airy.

I gazed around. I was still in the bathroom. Martha bent over me. I watched her crouch over my body—from above.

Wait a second! Was I really seeing my own body? From above?

I stared at the scene below me, unable to believe what I was seeing. My body lay in the tub. Its eyes were closed. It was covered in magic herbs.

But I wasn't inside my body anymore.

Pete had pushed *me* out!

He must have used the power of the spell to get rid of me completely!

Oh, no! Terror spread within me as I realized what had happened.

No! I thought. I'm—I'm a ghost!

I was floating outside my body. Martha didn't seem to see me. She thought I was still inside the body in the tub.

"Becky!" Martha cried. "Are you all right? Did it work? Becky?"

"Martha! I'm up here!" I yelled.

She didn't look up. She shook my old body by the shoulders. The eyes flew open. The mouth began to speak.

My voice came out. But not my words.

"It worked all right, Martha. Thanks for helping me—get rid of Becky."

Pete let my head drop back, shrieking with laughter. Martha screamed. She shrank back against the wall, horrified.

"What have I done!" she wailed. "Becky! Where are you?"

I shouted, "I'm up here! Just above you!"

But she didn't hear me.

"*I* can hear you, Becky." Pete spoke to me, using my own voice. "I'm a spirit like you. I know how to listen to other spirits. But Martha can't. You have no voice to talk to her with!"

He started laughing again. Martha stared around the room. "Becky!" she repeated. "Where are you?"

I didn't know what powers I had. I couldn't talk—but could I move things? I had no hands, but I had a kind of energy, like a force field.

I knocked over a bottle of shampoo.

"I saw that!" Martha shrieked. "Becky, was that you? Give me another sign."

I knocked over the hair conditioner.

Pete hauled my body out of the tub. "Nice try, Becky," he snarled. "But you're getting on my nerves, you know that? I can't believe you tried to kick me out! We were getting along so well!"

"Let me back in!" I demanded. "It's my body!"

"Not anymore. You hurt my feelings, Becky. No one ever tried to get rid of me like that before! So now you're kicked out of your body for good! It will last me until my birthday—when I get to pick out a new one.

"But once I do, your body will be empty. Like a seashell. Empty—and dead.

"You won't be able to get back inside it. You'll be a ghost forever—just like me! Ha-ha-ha!"

Chapter EIGHTEEN

"No!" I shrieked, filled with terror. "You can't do that! That's not how it works! I've heard the stories. You're not playing by the rules! The kids are supposed to get their bodies back after you tag someone else."

"I changed the rules, Becky—just for you!" Pete turned my voice into a nasty purr. It was my voice—but pure evil.

"The other kids never left their bodies completely. They stayed inside with me! *You're* the one who didn't play by the rules. You tried to kick me out! So now I'm keeping you out. Forever!"

"No!" I protested. I dove at my body. I tried to push my way inside.

But instead, I bounced right off my skin!

"I'll get in somehow," I vowed. I got a running start and tried to slam back inside.

Again, it didn't work. I bounced all the way up to the ceiling.

I wanted to cry with frustration. But I had no eyes and no tears to cry with!

"You can't do it!" Pete laughed again. He seemed to think this was hilarious. "It's my body! It's my body! Ha-ha-ha-ha-ha!"

He danced around crazily. Then he threw open the bathroom door and galloped away, shrieking like a maniac.

"Come back!" Martha screamed. "Becky! Pete! Whoever you are!" She stared, horrified, at my body as it raced down the hall.

"Martha, help me," I moaned. She couldn't hear me.

Martha glanced around the bathroom as if she were searching for me. "Becky? Are you still here?"

I threw the shampoo bottle at her. She peered in the direction I threw the bottle from.

"Becky, this is all my fault! I'm sorry. I guess I'm not a very good sorceress. I should stick to being Ben Franklin."

I could hear Pete in the kitchen, clanging pots and pans together. What's going to happen to my body now? I wondered.

Who knows what Pete will do with it?

And what's going to happen to *me*?

"Listen, Beck," Martha said. "We can't give up. I don't want to have Pete for a sister."

I opened the door to the medicine cabinet and slammed it shut to show I agreed.

"I've read a lot of books about ghosts," Martha said. "There must be something else we could try."

"Yeah?" I muttered. "Like what?"

Martha was thinking out loud. "What if you lured him into the cemetery? Maybe you can send him back to the grave!"

Yeah. Sure, I thought. How am I supposed to do that?

But Martha picked up her big book on magic and flipped through the pages. "Ah! Here it is!" She read for a moment, then glanced up. "Graves are supposed to have this strong spirit force. It's like a sucking action—it keeps the ghosts down in their graves. They find ways to get out, of course—but it's not easy. The force is pretty powerful. If you can just get Pete to lie on his own grave—maybe it will suck him out of your body and send him back to his coffin!"

I'll try anything, I thought. What have I got to lose?

No matter what Pete said about my being a ghost forever, I would find a way to get back into my body. I just had to!

"So, Beck? You want to try it?"

I grabbed Martha by the hair and made her look in the mirror. Then I pulled her hair up and down, making her head nod.

"Yes? Okay. You stick close to him. If he gets anywhere near the cemetery, you have to pin him on top of his grave. And, Becky—I think you should do it soon!"

"I know you're there, Becky," Pete growled. "Stop following me. There's nothing you can do."

It was almost midnight. Pete was sneaking my bike out of the garage. Going for a midnight bike ride.

He'd been running around like a maniac all day. He was tiring my poor body out. It was covered with bruises. And all I could do was watch him helplessly.

I couldn't wait to send him back to his grave.

He started pedaling wildly down the street. I flew after him.

"Coming with me, huh?" he grunted. "I think you have a crush on me!"

"That does it," I yelled. "You're going back to your grave, buddy. And I'll make sure you never get out again!"

"I don't think so, Becky baby," he replied, laughing hoarsely.

He sped down Fear Street. We approached the cemetery.

I tried to move the handlebars to the left. I wanted to steer the bike into the graveyard.

"Oh, no, you don't!" he cried. He fought me, pulling hard to the right. I pushed back, using all my strength.

Suddenly, I stopped pushing. But he was still pulling hard to the right.

"Whoa!" He lost his balance and fell off the bike—right in front of the cemetery.

"Get in there!" I cried. I flew down on him and started tickling him. I knew exactly where he'd be most ticklish. It was my body, after all.

"No!" he shrieked. "Stop it!" He started laughing helplessly. He crawled across the grass, trying to get away from me.

He crawled toward the cemetery. I fell on him again and tickled him some more.

"No! Please! It's torture!" he gasped. He struggled to get away from me—and crawled right through the cemetery gates.

I tickled him until he got weaker and weaker. I tickled him all the way to his grave.

He glanced back at the headstone. "No!" he cried. But he couldn't move. He was out of breath.

I pinned him down on the grave. "Now you'll pay," I promised. "Come on, spirit force! Suck him back to his coffin!"

"Becky, no!" he wailed.

The wind picked up. Soon it was howling, strong as a tornado.

I feel it, I thought. Martha was right. There is a force from the grave!

I felt it pulling from below, from underground. I kept Pete pinned down.

"Noooo!" he screamed. His eyes widened with terror.

He's scared, I thought. It must be working!

The force grew stronger, pulling down, down . . .

Suddenly, Pete broke out laughing. "Ha-ha-ha!"

I felt myself being sucked down.

"No!" I screamed. "Not me! *Him!*"

But something dragged me down, pulling, pulling . . .

I understood the horrible truth.

The force wasn't pulling Pete's spirit out of my body.

It was pulling *my* spirit—down into the grave!

Chapter NINETEEN

"**H**a-ha-ha!" Pete jumped up and laughed at me. "You tried to get rid of me again! But it won't work. I have a live body—the spirits can't get me! But you—you're doomed!"

He danced away, hooting and howling. I tried to follow him, to get away—but the force held me. It tugged on me, dragging me down.

"No!" I shouted. "I won't let this happen!"

I thought I heard voices in the wind. Ghostly voices, whispering, "Come down to us. Come down where you belong. In your grave!"

"NO!" I screamed. "I'm not a ghost!"

I gritted my teeth. I summoned up all my strength, every bit of stubbornness in me.

"Underground," the ghosts whispered. "Your home."

The ghosts pulled and pulled. I struggled to stay up, above the ground.

I turned my whole spirit into a force of resistance. I used all my energy. You can do it, Becky. You can do it!

"Join us . . . join us . . ." the ghosts coaxed.

"No!" I yelled. "NOOOOOOO!"

The wind suddenly stopped. *Whoosh!* My spirit flew up to the tops of the trees.

"I did it!" I cried. "I beat the force of the grave!"

I paused, calming myself. My spirit is really strong, I realized. But that was too close. I'm never going near a graveyard again!

I glanced around for Pete. No sign of him. He was probably out crashing my bike somewhere.

I didn't know what else to do, so I flew home. I hovered all night in Martha's room. It made me feel better, watching her sleep.

Since I had no body, I didn't need to sleep. It was just as well. I had a lot of thinking to do.

I glanced at the calendar on Martha's desk. It was June eighth. Pete's birthday was only two days away. In two days, I realized, Pete will walk my body to the Fear Street Woods. All the other kids will arrive. They'll play hide-and-seek.

Pete will tag someone. His spirit will leave my body. He'll torture some other poor kid for a year.

But then my body will be empty. I won't be able to get back in. I'll be dead!

I'm doomed! Just like Pete said!

I can't let that happen. I can't let Pete tag someone else.

As long as his spirit is in my body, he keeps it alive.

So I can't let him leave—until I figure out a way to get back inside myself.

And I have only two days.

By the time the sun rose, I had a plan.

If no one shows up for the game, I figured, Pete can't tag anyone.

And if he can't tag anyone, he can't leave my body. He can't let it die.

I'll make sure no one goes to the Fear Street Woods, I vowed. I'll scare them away.

It'll be easy. I'm a ghost, after all.

I'll haunt them.

Pete showed up at school the next day—in my body, of course.

What's he been doing all night? I wondered. My jeans were torn, there were leaves in my tangled hair, and my face was smudged with dirt. Plus he— or I—smelled funny.

The other kids stared and cleared a path for him. No one talked to him.

"What are you looking at?" he snarled at Darcy. "Go jump in a garbage pail."

Darcy gasped. "I can't believe I tried to be friends with you, Becky!"

"I can't believe I ever looked at your face without puking," Pete growled. He bent over and made fake puking noises. Then he laughed as Darcy stormed off.

"She's so gross," one boy murmured. The other kids agreed.

He's ruining me! I thought, horrified. No one will ever like me again!

I'm going to get you, Pete, I vowed. You won't get away with this.

I gathered my energy. Well, I thought. Here goes . . .

I flew down the hallway, opening lockers and slamming them shut. *Bang! Bang! Bang! Bang!*

The kids turned and stared. A few kids screamed.

"What's happening?" one girl cried. "Those lockers—they're opening by themselves!"

"I know what you're up to, Becky," Pete muttered. "It won't work!"

I stopped at one locker and threw all the books out onto the floor.

"Hey!" a boy yelled. "My books!" He hurried to pick them up.

"Ha-ha-ha!" Pete laughed nervously. "Pay no attention! It's only a practical joke! See you around!" He strutted off.

He's trying to confuse them, I realized. But that won't work for long.

"How'd she do that?" the kids asked. "She's crazy!"

I followed Pete to my science class. He sat in the back row, scowling. The girl he sat next to moved to another seat.

I noticed Mina in the corner, watching him.

The teacher, Mrs. Marvel, called the roll. "Adam Aronson."

"Here."

"Mina Baird."

"Here."

Pete sat quietly at his desk until the teacher called, "Becky Tabor."

"Dead!" Pete shrieked. He let out a shrill laugh.

"Very funny, Becky," Mrs. Marvel snapped.

I watched him make a fool of me for two more classes. I was biding my time until the period where I knew I could cause the most damage—lunch.

Pete dropped his tray at a table already crowded with kids. They stared while he poured milk into a glass. He dumped spoonfuls of sloppy joe into the milk and stirred. Then he stuck a straw into the glass and slurped.

Ugh. I hated to think of that stuff going into my stomach.

"You're disgusting!" a girl cried. All the kids at the table got up and moved.

I left Pete to play with his food and followed the other kids. I picked up an empty plate and hurled it like a Frisbee across the room. It smashed against the wall.

"Who did that?" Max asked.

Sorry to do this to you, Max, I thought. But it's for your own good.

I knocked his tray over. Milk, green beans, and sloppy joe splattered on the floor.

"Max!" Darcy screeched. "What did you do that for?"

"I didn't do it!" he insisted. "It—it fell by itself!"

"Sure it did," Laura said. "You probably threw that plate too."

No, he didn't, Laura, I thought. I grabbed Laura's spoon. I dipped it in chocolate pudding and flung the pudding at the wall.

"Laura!" Darcy gaped at her.

"I didn't do it!" Laura cried.

I picked up Darcy's milk carton. I let it float around Darcy's head for a minute.

"It's floating—by itself!" Laura gasped.

I poured the milk out slowly. Darcy screamed. Then I knocked over her tray, for the heck of it.

"Aaaaaahhhhh!" Darcy, Laura, and Max all leapt up from the table, screaming like crazy. A lunch supervisor stomped over to them.

"What's going on here?" she demanded. "Look at this mess!"

"We didn't do it!" Darcy and Laura clutched each other, terrified.

"Don't lie to me!" shouted the supervisor. "Go get the mop and clean this mess up!"

I snatched the supervisor's hairnet off her head. "Oh!" she shrieked. I plopped the net on Darcy's head.

"I didn't do it!" Darcy swore.

Then I picked up speed. I crashed around the lunchroom, toppling trays left and right. Soon the cafeteria was in chaos. Kids screamed and ran around in circles.

"A ghost!" Max shouted. "A ghost!"

"Calm down!" the supervisor roared. "Order! Order!"

No one could hear her over the din. The room was a total mess.

Pretty soon, kids were throwing food and knocking their trays over themselves. I didn't even have to do anything anymore. I floated above them, watching.

Pete sat calmly in the middle of it all, mixing a pea and pudding milk shake. And Mina stood in the corner, ignoring the mess around her. She eyed Pete warily, frowning.

Kids flooded the halls. "There's a ghost in the cafeteria!" they shouted.

My lunchtime work was done. Now, back to class.

As the kids settled into their seats, the principal, Mr. Emerson, spoke over the intercom.

"Students, I would like to ask you all to calm down," he ordered. "There is a rumor going around the school. I'm going to stop that rumor once and for all.

"There is no ghost in the cafeteria!" he declared. "I repeat—the cafeteria is not haunted!"

Some of the kids giggled.

"Something bad did happen there, however. It wasn't a ghost. It's called a food fight. And every student involved in that food fight will get detention for a week!"

The kids groaned. "He can't give detention to the whole seventh grade!" one girl protested.

"I want all students to remain calm and orderly," the principal finished. "That is all."

"There *was* a ghost!" Laura insisted. "I saw milk flying by itself!"

The class burst out laughing.

"Quiet!" The teacher, Mr. Silver, slammed a book on his desk. "Let's settle down."

Pete burst into the classroom and took a seat in the back.

"Becky Tabor, you're late," Mr. Silver snapped.

"Well, you're ugly," Pete shot back. "Personally, I'd rather be late."

A few kids snickered. Oh, boy, I thought. He's

really getting me in trouble. I'm going to have to switch schools after this.

Mr. Silver glared at Pete. "One more smart word from you and you're going to the principal's office."

"Don't worry," Pete said. "I'll say only stupid things from now on."

Mr. Silver narrowed his eyes at Pete. But he let it go.

"All right, people," he said. "Let's talk about the Civil War." He turned around to write something on the blackboard.

Crash! I knocked over the empty desk next to Pete.

Mr. Silver wheeled around. "All right. What happened here?" he demanded.

I knocked over a stack of books. I picked up a globe and floated it across the room.

"The ghost!" Max cried. "The ghost is back!"

"It's a trick!" Pete yelled. "It's just another trick!"

But no one believed him this time. Even Mr. Silver was shaking.

Kids were screaming and shouting. Some of them headed for the door.

"What's happening?" Laura wailed.

I'll tell you, I thought. I snatched the chalk out of Mr. Silver's hand.

I scrawled one word on the blackboard—PETE.

"Pete!" Max screamed. "Pete's back!"

There was an uproar as all the kids scrambled for the door. Even Mr. Silver hurried out of the room.

"You're wrong!" Pete shouted. "He's not back! Don't forget the game!"

"Shut up, Becky!" Laura snapped. "What do you know about it?" She grabbed her books and raced out of the room.

I heard panic and screaming out in the hall. "Pete's back! Pete's back!" the kids squealed.

Soon Pete and I were left alone in the empty classroom.

"You're really starting to bug me, you know that, Becky?" he said.

"Not as much as you bug me," I replied.

I flew through the halls, watching the panic. Word spread quickly. Pete was back. I could see the fear on the kids' faces.

I hope this works, I thought. They're scared. But are they so scared they won't show up for the game?

"Happy birthday to me, happy birthday to me!" Pete hummed. He was rummaging through my closet. "Let's see, what can I wear to my birthday party?" He pulled out my favorite minidress. Black with yellow and white daisies on it.

"Not really my style," Pete commented. "But I guess that's my fault for being stuck in a stupid *girl's* body."

"No! Not that dress!" I cried.

"It's your favorite, right?" Pete said. "Good. You'll want to be wearing your favorite dress—when you *die*."

"I *won't* die," I insisted. "No one is going to show up at your stupid game. You won't be able to tag anyone. You'll stay in my body—till I find a way to get you out!"

"You're wrong," Pete said. "They'll all show up. And then—you'll be doomed."

I followed him to the Fear Street Woods. No one was there. But it was still early.

My plan just has to work, I prayed. It has to!

But I won't know until the night is over.

Dusk settled over the woods. I waited in the eerie stillness.

What's going to happen tonight? I wondered.

Will anyone show up?

What if the others come? Pete will surely tag one of them.

And then—what will become of me?

Without a spirit, my body will die.

Will I be a ghost—forever?

Chapter TWENTY

It was completely dark now. So far, no kids had come to the woods.

I'm safe, I thought.

Then I heard voices. Oh, no.

"Are we the first ones here?" It was Darcy and Laura.

"Looks like it," Laura said. "Maybe no one else will show up."

"I'm not playing unless everybody else plays," Darcy said.

But then Max arrived, and Jeff. Mina came, and all the other twelve-year-olds in town. Including me. Or rather, including Pete—in *my* body.

"Ha-ha-ha!" Pete snickered at me. "I knew they'd show up. They're too scared not to! You lose again,

Becky!" He crept off into the woods to hide.

The kids huddled nervously together at the edge of the woods. I had scared them—I could see that. But not enough.

"What are we doing here?" Darcy asked. "Pete is back—he's going to tag one of us!"

"Yeah!" Jeff agreed. "Why don't we all leave?"

"We can't," Max reminded them. "*Especially* since Pete is back. Remember what happens if he doesn't tag someone on his birthday? Bad things start happening to *all* of us."

"That's right," Mina said softly. "We have to play even though we don't want to."

Everyone grew quiet. "When do we start?" someone whispered.

At last a man arrived. I recognized him as the gym teacher, Mr. Sirk. He waved his flashlight. The kids crowded around him.

"Welcome, kids." His voice was low and grave. "You all know why you're here."

The kids shuffled, murmured, and nodded.

"I was hoping this year would be different from the past," Mr. Sirk said. "We all thought Pete was gone for good. I had hoped that maybe, this year, Pete's birthday game would be all in fun.

"But—well, I'm sure you've all heard the rumor. People are saying that Pete is back. I don't know for sure if this is true. But, to tell you the truth, it wouldn't surprise me. I've lived in Shadyside for many years. Pete has always been around. No one has ever truly beaten him."

I will, I swore. I've got to. Or I'm a goner!

"I'm sure you all know the rules," Mr. Sirk said. "When I give the signal, you all run into the woods to hide."

He pointed to a big old tree. "That tree is home base. You must stay in the woods for at least half an hour. After that, start to make your way out. On your way, touch that tree and you're safe. But remember—for half an hour, no one is safe."

The kids stood perfectly still, listening.

"Pete's going to try to tag one of you—if he's out there." Mr. Sirk waved toward the dark, dark woods.

He's out there, all right, I thought. But he's not going to tag anyone—not if I can help it.

"If he tags you—" Mr. Sirk went on. "Well, you've all heard the stories. Good luck, kids. And be careful."

Mina held up a huge cake. It was decorated with twelve candles and *Happy Birthday, Pete*.

Max struck a match and lit the candles.

Everyone sang "Happy Birthday." They sang it like a funeral march.

This *feels* like a funeral, I thought grimly.

It better not be mine!

Suddenly, the candles blew out. The woods were deep black. The game began.

Everyone spread out into the woods. I tried to keep an eye on Pete, but he melted into the darkness. I flew around, searching for him. I wanted to stick close to him.

I heard Darcy whisper to Laura, "Who's Pete? We don't know what he looks like this year!"

Laura shrank back. "Maybe you're Pete!"

"I am not!" Darcy cried.

"How do I know?" Laura said. "Anyone could be him! I'm not going near anybody!"

Laura squealed and ran away from Darcy.

"Laura, wait!" Darcy cried. "I don't want to be alone out here!"

"Stay away from me!" Laura screamed.

Max ran past them. "How do you know Laura's not Pete?" he asked Darcy.

Darcy shuddered and backed away from him. "Or—or you, Max! I hate this game!"

Kids dashed nervously from tree to tree. At last, after flying over a grove of trees, I found Pete, hiding behind a bush, waiting for his first victim. I settled next to him.

"Leave me alone!" he snapped. "Go find somebody else to haunt! I've got work to do."

"So do I," I replied.

I stuck to him like a shadow. Jeff ran up to the bush.

Get away! Get away! I wanted to scream.

Pete burst out from behind the bush. He lunged for Jeff. Jeff yelped in terror. He managed to dodge Pete's hand.

"Becky is Pete!" Jeff shouted, hurrying away. "Everyone—listen! Becky is Pete!"

"Rats!" Pete snarled. "It's so much easier when they don't know."

He started running through the woods, growling like an animal. I stuck close by him. Kids scattered in his path.

"Grrooowwwl!" he roared. "Come out, come out, wherever you are!"

Something glowed near the bottom of a tree. One boy had worn his glow-in-the-dark sneakers. He was hiding behind the tree with only his shoes showing.

"Ah-ha," Pete murmured. "There's one."

He crept up to the tree. The boy didn't hear him.

No! I thought. I dashed up to the nearest branch and rattled it.

The boy looked around—and saw Pete coming.

"Help!" he shrieked. He ran away, disappearing into the shadows.

"Becky!" Pete grumbled. "You can help them all you want—it won't help *you*! Sooner or later I'm going to tag one of them—and you'll be gone forever! So quit following me!"

He stopped, pricking up his ears. Someone was

hiding in the bushes a few yards away. The bushes rustled a tiny bit.

"Ah-ha . . ." he murmured.

He sneaked up to the bushes. A girl suddenly jumped up. Mina!

"I'm going to get you!" Pete yelled.

"No!" Mina screamed. She dodged him and ran away. Pete scrambled after her.

Run, Mina! I thought. She hadn't been very nice to me, but she didn't deserve to be Pete's next victim.

Mina scurried through the dead leaves, darting from tree to tree. I shadowed Pete as he chased her. He was pretty fast—but Mina was faster.

Go, Mina, go! I cheered. I could tell that Pete was getting tired. Mina was getting away.

Maybe the half hour will pass before anyone is tagged, I hoped. Maybe they'll all touch base and get out safely.

Then Mina's foot caught on a root. She tripped and fell to the ground.

"All right!" Pete huffed. He closed in on her.

No! I screamed. I had to stop him!

"Arf! Arf!" I heard barking. I turned.

A dog! The same brown-and-white dog I hit with my bike! It skittered across Pete's path, stopping to sniff at Mina.

I had to do something—quick!

Mina struggled to get up. Pete reached out to tag her.

I grabbed the dog. Pete's hand was inches from Mina's back.

I shoved the dog in front of him.

"Nooooo!" Pete screeched. He tried to pull his hand back.

Chapter TWENTY-ONE

Too late. He tagged the dog!

"No!" Pete wailed again. "Not the dog!"

Mina and I stared as my body started shaking. Faster. Faster.

"What's happening?" Mina asked.

My body shook harder and harder, until it blurred in front of me.

"Who-o-o-a-a!" Pete stuttered.

With a whoosh, his spirit zoomed out of my body and into the dog!

Oh, no! I thought. What have I done?

Pete tagged someone—the dog. Now my body was empty. Pete had said it would die!

I won't let that happen, I vowed. I had to get myself back into my body—before it was too late!

My body stood empty, teetering, ready to collapse any second!

I summoned all my willpower. I called out, "Becky! Becky! Becky!"

I threw myself into the vacuum left by Pete's spirit. I rammed my way in. Nothing was going to keep me out!

"Becky, Becky, Becky!" I repeated.

Whoosh! A rush of wind. The air was pulling me, pulling me. I felt as if a vacuum cleaner were sucking me in.

The wind grew stronger, louder, shrieking like a witch. I had to make it! I had to get back to my body!

Chapter TWENTY-TWO

Suddenly, everything stopped.

No more wind. All was quiet.

I opened my eyes. Did it work? I thought. Do I have my body back?

And then I realized—*I opened my eyes!*

I had eyes again!

I looked at my hands. I touched my face. I pulled my own hair.

"Woo-hoo!" I shouted. I could talk! "I'm back!"

Mina touched my arm. "Becky? Is that you?"

"You touched my arm!" I cried. "I felt it! Isn't that cool?"

I touched her arm. "Look! I touched you!"

Mina laughed. But then she said, "Where's Pete?"

We both looked at the dog. "Aaawooo!" He howled and ran away.

"That poor dog is Pete now," I explained. "I made him tag the dog. Game over."

Mina and I ran out of the woods, yelling, "Olly olly oxen free!"

The kids crept out of their hiding places. "Is it over?" they asked, staring at me suspiciously. "Did he tag someone?"

"That little brown-and-white dog," Mina told them. "He tagged the dog. Spread the word."

Mina and I walked home down Fear Street. "Thank you," Mina said. "You saved me. If it weren't for you, I could be Pete right now!"

"Nobody should be Pete," I said. "In fact, I'd rather be a dog!"

"Ha-ha." Mina smiled. "Believe me, I know what it's like. My older brother was taken over by Pete three years ago. It was horrible!"

"Is he okay now?" I asked.

"He's all right, but he has terrible nightmares," she said.

We walked quietly for a few minutes. Then Mina added, "You must've thought I was pretty weird. I mean, following you around and stuff."

"I did," I admitted. "I thought you were Pete for a while!"

"That's why I was watching you so closely," she explained. "I suspected Pete was in you. I saw my brother go through it. I know the signs. Plus, you're new. And you really were acting strangely. But I had to be sure. That night when I followed you to the cemetery—that's when I was sure."

I laughed. "I'm so glad this is all over. We'll have to make sure to tell everyone to stay away from that dog. Pete used him to lure me into the cemetery—that's how he got me. We can't let that happen again."

"I'll warn everyone," Mina promised.

When I got home, I took a nice, long bath. My body was a little scratched up, but basically okay. I went to bed and fell asleep right away. And I slept like a baby.

Before I knew it, Mom was calling, "Becky! Breakfast!"

I leapt out of bed. I was starving—I couldn't wait to eat normal food again!

I threw on some clothes and dashed downstairs, whistling. Mom set a plate of pancakes in front of me.

"You're in a good mood today," she said.

"Yep," I replied.

Martha stared at me. I waved at her.

"'Early to bed and early to rise,'" I quoted in Ben Franklin code, "'makes a man healthy, wealthy, and wise.'"

She broke into a smile. "'No pain, no gain!'" she said.

Dad came in and poured himself some orange juice. "Good morning, everyone." He stood in front of me and opened his arms wide. "You going to throw any food at me today, Becky? Come on, let's get it over with." He patted his chest. "Right here, Beck—lob a pancake right at my heart. And make sure it's sticky with syrup."

"I'm not going to throw anything at you, Dad," I assured him. "I don't feel like it."

"That's good to know. So I can relax and eat my breakfast?"

"Go ahead."

I gobbled down my pancakes and asked for more.

"Well, well." Mom cheerfully refilled my plate. "I'm glad to see you're more like your old self again, Becky. I was beginning to worry about you."

"Maybe it was that weird hide-and-seek game they play here," Dad offered. "I'll bet you were nervous about it. I would be."

"I'm glad it's over, that's for sure," I said.

"Did you hear something?" Martha asked.

I listened. I heard a muffled whine, and scratching at the kitchen door.

"What could that be?" Mom wondered.

I went to the back door. I looked out the window.

"Who's there?" Dad asked.

I shrugged. I didn't see anyone.

I opened the door—and gasped. There at me feet stood a brown-and-white dog.

Pete!

Chapter TWENTY-THREE

Mom, Dad, and Martha gathered around to see the dog. "He's kind of cute," Mom commented.

The dog growled.

"But he's not very nice," Mom added.

"I'll bet he's hungry," Dad said.

I gazed into the dog's eyes. They glowered at me crazily.

It's Pete, all right, I thought.

Even though Pete had given me nothing but trouble, I felt kind of sorry for him.

I gathered some scraps from the fridge and took them outside. I set them down. The Pete dog gobbled them up and begged for more.

He needs me, I realized. All the kids know he's Pete—so nobody will feed him or take care of him.

I felt sorry for the dog. I mean, it wasn't his fault that his body got taken over by Pete. Why should he starve, just because Pete was in him?

So I decided to keep the dog. That way, also, I could keep an eye on Pete. I could make sure he never took over another kid's body.

I still have him. My parents think I'm strict with him. They don't understand. I have to keep Pete in line.

Actually, Pete behaves pretty well. Whenever he's bad, I just threaten to toss him back in the grave.

I think he'd rather be a dog than a ghost. Wouldn't you, Pete?

Too bad he can't talk. I wonder what he's thinking.

Stupid girl. Being a dog isn't exactly what I had in mind. But I'm getting used to it. And I kind of like dog food. It's better than that lousy cafeteria food any day.

Of course, it's not as tasty as worms—but then, I'm a dog. I can still eat worms whenever I want.

Good dog, Pete. Good dog.

Turn the page to sneak a peek
at what's coming up next!
The Tale of the Blue Monkey

THE TALE OF THE
BLUE MONKEY

Coming in April 1998

"**D**on't open that door!" I yelled to the boy walking through a dark, gloomy house. "There's a killer behind it!"

"Amanda, chill!" My brother Danny turned to me and rolled his eyes.

We were watching an old episode of "The Twilight Zone." It was one of Danny's favorite TV shows. Just hearing the theme music gave me the creeps. But I made myself watch it with Danny to prove to both of us that I wasn't chicken.

Bess, our sitter for the weekend, had gone to bed half an hour before. She said Danny and I could stay up for a while on one condition—no fighting.

I nudged Danny. "You think that blue monkey doll is really buried in the backyard?" I asked him. "You think we've walked over its grave a thousand times without realizing it?"

He shrugged. "What difference does it make?" he asked. "Even if it's there, you're way too chicken to go outside and dig it up."

"I am not!" I insisted.

"You are too," he insisted. "You even thought that lame story about the curse was scary. Chicken!"

I glared at him. "Stop calling me chicken!"

"*Cluuck, cluuck, cluuck!*" Danny flapped his arms at his sides as if they were chicken wings. "Let's hear it for Amanda, the Amazing Chicken Girl!"

I felt my face growing hot. I *hated* it when Danny called me that!

I'm *not* chicken!" I declared. I hopped off the couch. "I'm not! And I'll prove it!"

A full moon shone in the sky as I hurried toward the garden shed. I slid open the door. Half a dozen shovels hung in a row on the wall. I lifted off the biggest one. It weighed a ton.

Too heavy for me. I put it back and took a smaller shovel.

I walked out to the yard again. By now, my nerve was starting to leak away.

I tried to tell myself that it was no big deal. Lots of people probably dug up their backyards in the middle of the night. And nothing ever happened to them. Right?

Yeah, sure.

Then I thought of Danny making clucking noises. Flapping his arms.

I had to do this. I didn't have a choice.

I carried the shovel over to the biggest tree in our yard, a huge, ancient oak. I placed its blade against the ground and put my foot on its edge, just the way I'd seen Omar, the gardener, do.

"Boo!" Danny yelled from behind me.

I jumped. The shovel fell to the ground.

But I didn't let myself scream.

I gave Danny a furious look. "Shhhhh!" I hissed. I nodded toward the house. "If Bess catches us out here in the middle of the night, you'll be in as big trouble as me."

"She won't hear a thing," Danny blustered. "She's old. She's probably hard of hearing." But I noticed he was whispering.

I turned my back on him and started digging for real. I lifted up big hunks of dirt and grass.

"Give up, Amanda," Danny whispered. "You have no idea where the monkey is buried. If there really is a blue monkey."

"Bess said it was next to a tree," I reminded him. "And there are only four trees in the backyard."

"Dad's going to ground you if he finds out you dug up his lawn looking for some stupid hundred-year-old toy," Danny said.

I shrugged. "He'll just blame it on the gophers."

The hole was about two feet deep now. And there definitely weren't any blue monkeys in it. So I stepped two paces to the right and started again.

As I pushed the shovel into the ground, the blade hit something hard.

My heart thudded in my chest. "Hey, I found it!" I whispered to Danny. I heaved up a chunk of Dad's precious lawn—and saw a big rock.

"Oh, yeah, that really looks like a toy monkey," Danny scoffed. "Nice going, Amanda!"

I did my best to ignore him and kept digging.

By the time I'd started my sixth hole, I'd worked up a sweat. "This is harder than I'd thought," I admitted. "You know, if you dug, too, it'd go faster."

"Not a chance." Danny shook his head. "I bet Bess made up the whole story about the blue monkey anyway." He rubbed his hands up and down over his arms. "It's getting cold out here. Come on. Let's go inside. I want to work on my model plane."

I gazed down at my hands. They were covered with blisters. The muscles in my back ached like anything.

I sighed. "Okay. I'll dig around the other trees tomorrow night."

I hung up the shovel in the shed. Tomorrow I'd ask Bess for a few more details about where the blue monkey was buried.

Then my brother's terrified scream echoed through the night.

"Aaaaaaaaaaaaaaaaaaaaaaaaaaaaaaah!"

I froze. "Danny?" I cried. "Where are you?"

My voice shook with fear.

The blue monkey! Had it gotten Danny?

"I—I'm over here," Danny called.

I let out a sigh. At least he was alive!

I peered in the direction of his voice. I came from

the base of the big oak tree. But all I could see was a dark shape on the ground.

I ran over to the shape. It was Danny. He was sitting on the ground, holding his leg.

"What happened?" I demanded.

"My foot is caught in one of these stupid gopher holes," he moaned.

"Can you get up?" I asked.

Danny shook his head. "It's stuck," he said. "Really stuck."

I crouched down next to Danny. "Wow, this is some gopher hole," I remarked. His leg had disappeared in the ground almost up to his knee.

"Wiggle your foot around," I suggested. "Maybe it'll loosen up."

Danny shook his head again. "I think it's caught in some tree roots or something. It won't budge."

"I'll get a shovel," I decided. I jumped up. "Don't move."

"Ha ha," Danny called after me as I ran to the shed.

I came back and started digging away the ground around Danny's leg. Luckily, the moon came out from behind the clouds, so I could really see what I was doing.

"Try now," I ordered, offering him a hand.

Danny gripped my outstretched hand and I heaved. His foot slid out of the deep hole. He hopped a few times, gaining his balance, and caught himself against the tree.

"Whoa," he groaned, rubbing his ankle. "Lucky for you I didn't break my leg. It would have been all your fault."

I rolled my eyes. "You're welcome."

Danny began limping toward the house. I bent down for one last look at the hole. What could he have caught his foot on?

And then I saw it.

A squared-off shape. One corner glinted in the moonlight.

It definitely wasn't a rock.

"Hey! What's this?" I grabbed the shovel and poked around in the hole. "Something's down there, Danny."

"Dig it up," Danny ordered.

I was too excited to think about the blisters on my hands. I dug like crazy.

At last the rectangular thing was uncovered. I knelt down. With both hands, I reached into the hole and pulled out a container. It was metal, about the size of a shoe box.

I glanced up at Danny.

His eyes met mine.

I could tell he was wondering the same thing I was.

What was in the box?

* * *

"Let me see." Danny grabbed the box from me.

My heart was racing. I wanted him to rip off the lid. But at the same time, I was afraid.

Danny brushed off some dirt and read the faint letters on the old tin box: "Onida's Crispy Crackers." He handed me the box. "Here, Amanda," he said. "Have a cracker."

I giggled nervously and held the box up.

"Open it!" Danny urged.

"You think it's the monkey?" I asked. My heart pounded with excitement. And fear.

"We'll never know if you don't open it," Danny snapped.

I shook the box gently.

Something clanked inside.

It definitely wasn't crackers.

I ran a finger over the lid. "Let's open it in the morning," I suggested. Nothing was as scary in the bright light of day.

Danny snorted. He grabbed the box out of my hands and yanked off the lid.

"Tah-dah!" he cried.

I gasped.

The blue monkey lay in the box.

Its face, hands, and feet had been carved out of wood. The rest of its body was covered with thick blue fur. It wore a tattered black vest. Attached to its small wooden hands was a pair of tiny gold cymbals.

The monkey doll stared up with one coal black eye. The other eye was missing. It lay unmoving in the box as if it were in a coffin.

It seemed to be glaring at me.

A chill ran down my back.

I swallowed. I glanced from the monkey doll to Danny.

"What if Bess's story is true?" I whispered.

"Then you're cursed!" Danny said gleefully. "Just like the little girl in the story!"

"Well, if I'm cursed, so are you!" I cried.

"No way." Danny shook his head. "You dug up the box—not me. The monkey is yours. It belongs to you. You're definitely doomed!"

"You opened the lid," I reminded him. "You saw the monkey first."

Danny ignored me. "Cursed, cursed, cursed," he chanted. "Amanda is cursed!"

I suddenly felt tired. My muscles ached from digging and my blistered hands hurt. "I'm going in," I told Danny. "Here." I held out the blue monkey to him.

He dodged away.

Hah!

"What's the matter?" I sneered. "Scared?"

"Who, me?" Danny glared at me. He grabbed the

monkey by one ear and whisked it out of the box. "I'm taking it inside so we can ask Bess about it tomorrow." And he started for the house.

"Why ask about it if you don't believe in curses anyway?" I challenged.

Danny grinned at me. "Hey—what do I know?"

We took off our muddy shoes and left them on the back porch. Then we went inside.

As we walked through the dark den, Danny tossed the blue monkey on the couch. He ran up the stars.

I followed. As I started up the stairs, I glanced back at the monkey.

I gasped.

Its one black eye was glowing an evil orange in the dark.

A second later I realized that the orange glow was just a reflection from the hall light. "Whew," I muttered.

It's not evil, I told myself. It's just a toy.

Right?

About R. L. Stine

R.L. Stine is the best-selling author in America. He has written more than one hundred scary books for young people, all of them bestsellers.

His series include *Fear Street, Ghosts of Fear Street*, and the *Fear Street Sagas*.

Bob grew up in Columbus, Ohio. Today he lives in New York City with his wife, Jane, his son, Matt, and his dog, Nadine.

Don't Miss

R.L.Stine's

Ghosts of Fear Street #29

THE TALE OF THE
BLUE MONKEY

Amanda and Danny's babysitter loves to tell them scary stories. Like the one about a creepy toy monkey. It brought a terrible curse down on an entire family. And now, the legend says, the blue monkey is buried in the Mullers' own backyard!

Danny dares Amanda to search the yard for the blue monkey. What's the harm? She doesn't believe the story is true—does she?

It turns out the monkey really *is* there. And Danny and Amanda find it.

Does that mean the curse is going to find *them?*